Cloak Games: Thief Trap

Jonathan Moeller

Published by Azure Flame Media, LLC

Cover design by Clarissa Yeo

ISBN: 1515266036
ISBN-13: 978-1515266037

EPIGRAPH

We hang the petty thieves and appoints the great ones to public office.

-Aesop

OTHER BOOKS BY THE AUTHOR

Child of the Ghosts

Ghost in the Flames

Ghost in the Blood

Ghost in the Storm

Ghost in the Stone

Ghost in the Forge

Demonsouled

Soul of Tyrants

Soul of Serpents

Soul of Dragons

Soul of Sorcery

Soul of Skulls

Soul of Swords

CHAPTER 1
MASTER

One of the earliest things I remember is watching the entire United States Congress commit suicide on national television.

I don't know how old I was. Five years old, probably. I do remember that it was my first day of preschool, so I was most likely five. The teacher started the day by leading us through the Pledge of Allegiance, so we put our right hands upon our hearts and pledged allegiance to the flag of the United States of America, and to the High Queen of the Elves that protected the Republic for which it stood, one nation under God, indivisible, with security, order, and duty for all.

Then the teacher – her name was Miss Culpepper, I remember – had us sit on the floor, powered up the projector, and showed us the video clip. Later I learned that it was one of the High Queen's initial edicts after the Conquest three hundred years ago, that children on their first day of school should watch this video.

It was a clip from Year One of the Conquest, or 2013 AD according to the old calendar. It came from one of the old news networks, and showed the chambers of the United States Congress in Washington. Rows of desks and chairs faced the speaker's podium, and American flags hung on the back wall.

Tarlia, the High Queen of the Elves, stood there, surrounded by her chief nobles and commanders. She had long red-gold hair and eyes like discs of blue fire, and her pale face was so beautiful that it frightened me. The High Queen wore silvery battle armor that could deflect bullets, yet somehow clung to the curves of her body. A silver diadem studded with glowing white gems rested upon her brow, and she held a sword in her right hand. Her left hand flickered with ghostly light as she called upon her magic.

Under the command of her magic, one by one the Congressmen marched to the center of the floor, looked into the camera, lifted a gun to their temples, and blew out their brains. Some of them sobbed and begged for mercy. Some of them fought, shouting threats at the High Queen and her nobles, who gazed back impassively. None of Congressmen could resist her magic, and one by one they killed themselves.

You can imagine the effect this had on a room full of preschoolers.

By the end of the video, most of the class was crying. One of the other girls – I think her name was Melinda or Melissa or Melanie, something with an M – threw up on herself. Miss Culpepper and her aide hastened forward to clean her up.

I didn't cry. I just watched the video.

I suppose there might have been something wrong with me even then.

"I know that was very upsetting, children," said Miss Culpepper once all three branches of the United States government had killed themselves and ended the video, "but you shouldn't cry about it. Do you know why?"

We shook our heads. One of the boys, a fat child named Michael, raised a tentative hand.

"Because…the High Queen said so?" said Michael.

"Yes," said Miss Culpepper, smiling with approval. "That's right. Those were bad people, Michael. They were in charge of our country, but they were very wicked men and women. They stole from the people, lied and cheated and did many bad things. The High Queen brought justice to Earth. The President and Congress we have now are good men and women because they fear the High Queen, and know that she will punish anyone who mistreats her subjects." She turned her sunny smile toward the class. "And we are all the High Queen's subjects. Can anyone else tell me some of the good things the High Queen and her nobles have done for us?"

For a moment no one said anything, and then another boy raised his hand. "She…she stopped wars?"

"That's correct," said Miss Culpepper. "Before the Conquest, bad men could start wars with each other whenever they wanted. Our High Queen does not allow that now. Anyone else?"

A girl raised her hand. "She…brought us magic?"

"Correct," said Miss Culpepper, her smile widening. "Before the Conquest, no one on Earth could use magic. Now many people can learn magic, and help the High Queen defend our world from our enemies."

"My papa can use magic!" said another boy. "He's in the Wizards' Legion!"

His enthusiasm upset me. My father was in the Legion, too, and I wasn't as happy about it. I hadn't seen him in nearly a year. I had stopped crying myself to sleep, but my baby brother and mother hadn't.

"If the High Queen's magic is so strong," I said, "why does she need the Legion to fight her enemies…"

I had a smart mouth back then, too.

Miss Culpepper thought so as well. Before the sentence got all the way out of my mouth, she crossed the classroom and slapped me hard, once on the right cheek and again on the left. It was the first time (though not the last), someone had ever hit me, and I gaped up at her in astonishment.

"Shame, Nadia Moran!" said Miss Culpepper. "Shame on you! That is elfophobic, and elfophobia is ignorant and shameful! The Elves have done so much for us, and to question the High Queen is wrong! You should be ashamed of yourself."

Everyone was staring at me. I didn't know what to do, so I burst into tears. After school, I had to write "I will not question the High Queen and insult Elves" fifty times on the whiteboard. I managed to get to the thirty-ninth repetition before the hand cramps made me stop, and Miss Culpepper had mercy on me and let my mother drive me home.

I didn't like preschool very much.

Considering what happened later, I wish I had been able to stay longer.

###

That day is one of the first three things I can remember clearly. The other two are less pleasant.

My father was indeed in the Wizards' Legion, trained as an elemental wizard and recruited to fight in the High Queen's wars. The Elves might have forbidden human nations to war amongst themselves, but that did not stop the High Queen from fighting her enemies, for she had many enemies.

The Archons were chief among them.

As I later learned, the High Queen and her followers were exiles from the Elven homeworld. Tarlia had been overthrown by a group of rebels who called themselves the Archons, and the High Queen had fled with her loyalists and their armies into the Shadowlands, the paths between the worlds, and found themselves upon Earth. So the High Queen and her nobles raised armies from the conquered humans, and fought against the Archons in the paths of the Shadowlands between the worlds.

Except the laws of nature did not function in the Shadowlands as they did on Earth. Or at least the laws of physics, anyway. Magic worked in the Shadowlands, but electronics did not. Two minutes in the Shadowlands would destroy any electronic device. Gunpowder didn't work either, and nor did most explosives or internal combustion engines. So the armies of Her Majesty the High Queen trained to fight the way the men of the Middle Ages would have fought, with sword and spear and arrow and horse.

My father was one of those men. The Elves kept the greatest secrets of their magic to themselves, but they taught human wizards the spells of lesser elemental magic, fire and water and wind and earth. That made the Wizards' Legion of the High Queen valuable, but it also made the wizards into targets, and the Archons had allies from other worlds in the Shadowlands, allies with terrible weapons.

One of those weapons wounded my father, and it passed a disease called frostfever into his blood. Before he fell sick, he unknowingly passed it to my mother and my baby brother Russell, who would have been only a few months old at the time. I would have died with them. Maybe I should have died with them.

But some humans are naturally immune to frostfever, and I was one of them. Lucky me.

I remembered standing in the Seattle hospital, crying next to my parents' beds as they died, crying because I didn't know what to do. Crying because Russell was still alive, and I knew that he was going to die soon.

And I didn't know what was going to happen to me next.

The High Queen had kept the Constitution of the United States in place, including the Thirteenth Amendment, which banned slavery. However, the laws of the United States only applied to humans, not to Elves. Orphan children, or unwanted children, were often sold to Elven nobles. Even as a child, I had heard the horror stories, half true, half urban legend, of what happened to the slaves of Elven nobles.

After the orderlies wheeled my parents' bodies away, I stood over the little incubator holding Russell, watching him shiver as the frostfever burned through him, waiting for him to die.

A boot clicked against the polished floor of the hospital, and I looked up, expecting to see one of the nurses coming.

Instead an Elf walked towards me, and I went rigid with fear.

He was old. Elves can live a really long time, a thousand years or more, but this Elf looked older than that. He was tall and thin, his face gaunt and grim, his hair gray and close-cropped, his eyes like glittering chips of blue ice, his ears tall and pointed. His lips and fingernails had a peculiar blue tinge to them, the way you see in elderly people with heart trouble, and everything about him seemed cold. He wore the gold-trimmed black robe of an Elven archmage, and the ornamented red cloak favored by Elven nobles. At the age of five, I didn't know any of that – but I realized that I stood before an Elf of great power.

And he looked right at me with those cold, dead eyes.

"Well," said the Elf, his voice a deep rasp, "here you are."

I stared at him, too frightened to know what to do.

The Elf reached down and cupped my chin, forcing me to at him. His hands felt cold, and his fingers seemed to dig into my face.

"Yes," he murmured. "I see. Tell me. Where are your parents?"

I said nothing, and the fingers tightened, pain flashing through my jaw.

"Where are your parents?" said the Elf again, his calm never wavering.

"Dead," I whispered. "The frostfever took them."

"And the infant?" said the Elf. "Your brother?"

"He has the frostfever too," I said. "He's going to die next."

The Elf smiled for the first time. It was a sardonic smile, as cold as the rest of him. "Is he, now? Are you so sure of that, little girl?"

Anger spiked within me. "He is going to die! My parents died! No one could save them!" I wrenched free of his cold grasp and glared up at him. "Maybe the stupid Elves with their stupid magic could have saved them, but they didn't! I…"

The Elf simply stared at me, and I fell silent. Belatedly, my five-year-old brain realized that displaying elfophobia in front of an Elven noble was stupid. Miss Culpepper would have slapped me for elfophobia, but in hindsight she had a good reason for it. The Elves, especially Elven nobles, did not tolerate insults from their human subjects. The Elf lord could have killed me then and there, and the High Queen's law would have been on his side.

"Go on," I said. "Kill me. See if I care. My mom and dad are dead anyway. You can't make me any deader than that."

Yes, I did indeed have a smart mouth already.

The Elf kept staring at me, and I stared back, waiting for him to kill me. I didn't want to show any fear, but I could not stop myself from crying. Too much had happened already.

Then, to my utter astonishment, he chuckled.

"Then you do have some spirit," said the Elf. "Excellent. I would have preferred that the male carry the spark…but you may serve as well."

I blinked. "Spark?"

"Ah," said the Elf. "I forget how ignorant the young ones are. The spark. I shall show you."

Again his cold fingers clamped around my jaw, and this time ghostly blue fire danced around his hand. Fresh terror surged through me, and I would have screamed for the nurses and the doctors, but they would have stood by and let the Elf do whatever he wanted. But the strange cold fire did not burn me, and suddenly I felt it inside of my mind. I also felt the Elf's fingers reaching into my thoughts, sinking deeper and deeper.

It was a loathsome feeling, and the terror redoubled. Anger rose alongside the fear, and the scream burst from my lips. Without quite knowing how, I shoved against the intrusion inside my head, like pushing away a blanket.

The blue fire flickered and went out.

The Elf smiled his cold smile and withdrew his hand.

For a moment I could do nothing but gape in sheer astonishment. There had been a fire around his hand, and I had put it out with my mind. Nothing in my life had prepared me for something like this, and I struggled to understand it.

"The spark," said the Elf. "The inborn magical ability. A talent, if you prefer. Once it was extremely rare among your race. Then the High Queen opened the gates to the Shadowlands and we came here, and piercing Earth's umbra seemed to break some sort of protective shell around your world. Consequently, the spark has become much more common among humans. It would be a fascinating experiment to track the rate of the spark's progression in your population, though I have no interest in the matter." The cold smile turned a bit indulgent. "But you have no idea what I'm talking about, do you?"

"No," I whispered, my eyes turning back to Russell in his incubator.

"Perhaps you soon will," said the Elf.

"I don't care," I said. "Go away and leave me alone. I don't care about your stupid magic. I don't care about anything."

"Lies," said the Elf. "You care about the infant."

"He's going to die," I said, staring at Russell's small, limp form.

"My magic can save him," said the Elf.

I looked up at the tall figure in black and gold.

"It can?" I said.

"The frostfever inflicted by the blades of the frost giants is a deadly ailment, beyond the powers of your physicians and their machines," said the Elf. "Even for magic, it is a difficult cure, spread over many years, yet not beyond the skill of an archmage. It is in my power to cure your brother."

I stared at him, caught somewhere between hope and disbelief. I had a smart mouth…but I also had a suspicious mind, too. "Why? Why would you do that? Why would an Elf care about my brother?"

"I care nothing for your brother," said the Elf. "You, though…I have a great deal of work for you. I could simply buy you both as slaves. Yet given the nature of the work I require from you, that would be a foolish strategy. A slave is a tool that always betrays his master's work. No, I require your willing cooperation."

"To do what?" I said, baffled.

"In time," said the Elf. "In time. Do you understand what I am proposing?"

"I…I think so," I said.

"Then say it in your own words."

"You'll use your magic to heal Russell," I said, "if I do what you tell me to do."

"Precisely," said the Elf archmage, leaning closer to me. "Do you know what I will do to you if you disobey me or betray me?"

"You'll kill us both," I said.

"Of course not," said the Elf. "That would be inelegant. No, the spell necessary to cure frostfever shall require twenty different castings, one cast every year. Should you disobey me, should you betray me, I shall simply withhold my power, and your brother shall die."

I looked at the Elf, and I was frightened. I saw the power there, the cruelty. Even at the age of five, I knew that this was not a good man. I wanted to cry. I wanted to run to my mom and dad. But they were dead, and I was all that Russell had left. If I did nothing, he would die.

I couldn't let that happen.

"All right," I whispered.

The Elf raised an eyebrow. "I'm sorry?"

I swallowed and squared my shoulders. "I…I will do what you say, if you make Russell better. Please, Lord Elf." I remembered some of the manners Miss Culpepper had attempted to beat into my head. A human was always to address an Elf he did not know as Lord Elf, even if the Elf was not noble-born.

The Elf snorted. "You do have a modicum of manners, then. We shall have to work on that. What is your name, child?"

"Nadia," I said. "Nadia Moran."

"I am Morvilind," said the Elf, "an archmage of the Elven nation and a Knight of House Tamirlas, vassal to Lord Tamirlas, the Duke of Milwaukee. You may address me as Lord Morvilind, or as 'my lord', as you prefer." The cold blue eyes seemed to sink into me. "Now, Nadia Moran. Are you ready to follow my commands?"

I tried to work moisture into my mouth. I was only five years old, but I had the sense that I was about to make an irrevocable choice. Yet I was only five, and I could not articulate my fears.

Besides. Morvilind could help Russell. That was all that mattered. That was the only thing that could matter.

"Yes," I said, "my lord Morvilind."

"Good," said Morvilind. "Let us begin at once. I shall speak with the doctors and secure your release, and I suppose one of my human men-at-arms can take care of the infant. One of the childless ones, I expect."

"What?" I said. Morvilind gave me a look that was just short of a glare. "I mean…Lord Morvilind. Won't Russell be with me?"

"Of course not," said Morvilind. "Child, you and I have a great deal of work to do."

###

I had no idea what Morvilind wanted with me.

At the time, I guessed he wanted to put me to work in his mansion. When I was a child, there were a lot of cartoons on TV about orphaned girls going to work in an Elven lord's manor, gaining his approval through hard and industrious work, and then marrying one of the lord's handsome human men-at-arms. The show usually ended with an epilogue set twenty years later as the protagonist watched with proud eyes as her son joined her lord's service as a man-at-arms himself, ready to fight for the High Queen's honor in the paths of the Shadowlands.

In retrospect, I watched a lot of stupid TV as a child.

Anyway, that was what I expected. Scrubbing floors, cleaning pots, vacuuming carpets. That sort of thing.

Instead, two things happened.

First, before we even left the hospital, a physician visited, and gave me a drug that induced unconsciousness. When I awoke, I had a sharp pain in my chest and back, accompanied by a nasty bruise and a bandage. Morvilind informed me that he had drawn out a vial of heart's blood, and with his magic he could use that blood to find me anywhere in the world or the Shadowlands if I ran. And with that vial of blood, his magic could kill me from any distance as easily as crushing a cherry in his fist.

That should demonstrate the overall tone of our relationship.

Second, Morvilind started teaching me a variety of peculiar things.

We left Seattle, and he took me to his mansion. As a vassal of the Duke of Milwaukee, he had an estate in a little lakeside town called Shorewood a few miles north of Milwaukee. My parents and Russell and I had lived in a small two-bedroom house in Seattle, and Morvilind's mansion was so large that it boggled my mind. It was a sprawling pile of marble and glass and wood, built in the Elven style with a fine view of Lake Michigan. I looked at the house with dismay, wondering how long it would take me to scrub all those floors and wash all those windows.

Instead, I had tutors, some of them human, a few of them Elven.

In the mornings, I learned things most grade school children would have learned. Math and reading and lessons in English and Chinese and Spanish, the three most common human languages in the United States. I also learned High Elven, the language of government and law, and the use of computers. All the subjects were of a practical or technical nature. No history, no science, no art, no religion.

Then, in the afternoons and evenings, Morvilind's tutors taught me things I suspected grade school children in the United States generally did not learn.

First, there was a great deal of physical training. A hard-bitten man who had the look of a former man-at-arms made me run laps in a gym, over and over again, a little further every day. He also taught me how to lift weights, and made me do sets on days I did not run. Another man taught me self-defense, how to fight with my arms and legs and how to get away from an attack.

I learned other things. How to break into a computer illegally, whether I sat in front of it or accessed it over the Internet. How to open locks and safes and windows without being detected. How to use security systems, cameras and alarms and the like, and their weaknesses and vulnerabilities.

There were endless tests. I had to open a lock, or hack a computer, or pick the pocket of a man unseen. There were no grades. If I failed a test, one of the instructors beat me across the shoulders and hands with a leather belt. It never broke the skin or raised welts, but God it hurt. If I failed too many times, Morvilind himself came to see me, and spoke of how disappointed he would be if Russell died of frostfever because of my failures.

That drove me on.

I pushed myself endlessly, desperate and frightened. The failures grew fewer and fewer. By the time I turned twelve, I suppose there were few people who knew as much as I had learned about locks and security systems and hacking and traps. More and more, I wondered what Morvilind was training me to become. Some kind of soldier, maybe? That seemed unlikely. The High Queen forbade human women from serving in her armies. A woman's duty was to birth more sons and daughters for the defense of Earth from the Shadowlands, and a woman who died in battle could not birth children.

So what did Morvilind want with me? Why go to so much effort?

At the age of twelve a different set of lessons began.

Morvilind's hard-bitten retainers taught me to use weapons. Knives, pepper spray, stun guns, and firearms. As much as I hated my teachers, I really enjoyed shooting. It took discipline and focus and concentration, and there was something deeply satisfying about putting a bullet through a target from forty yards away. Certainly it was much more efficient than fighting with a knife.

I had another set of teachers. Women, this time, mostly middle-aged. They taught me about clothing and makeup and manners, how to carry myself, how to dress myself. All the things my mother would have taught me, I suppose, had she lived. I hit puberty around that time, and they taught me how to deal with some of adulthood's messier aspects.

I didn't particularly enjoy that.

And then, to my astonishment, Lord Morvilind himself became one of my teachers.

"It is time," he said, standing in the training room in his mansion, looking at the treadmills and weights with disdain. "You were too young to learn the power when we first met. Now that you have entered into what passes for adulthood among humans, you are ready."

With those words, he began instructing me in the use of magic.

His training focused upon the magic of illusion. Spells to create images, spells to alter the minds of others. Later I learned that the High Queen had forbidden humans from learning any kind of magic save that of the four elements, that any human who learned spells of illusion magic or mind magic was subject to summary execution. Morvilind did not share this little detail until later, but once he did, he never shut up about it, harping that if the Inquisition or the archmagi or the Wizards' Legion or even the Department of Homeland Security learned what I could do, they would kill me on sight. And then, with no need for my services, he would not be obliged to continue his annual spells for Russell's treatment.

Needless to say, I never breathed a word about my magic to anyone.

Nevertheless, I enjoyed learning to wield magic. The power, Morvilind said, came from the Shadowlands, radiated from it the way that heat and light came from the sun. Previously only a trickle had reached Earth, which was why true magic had been so rare in human history prior to the Conquest. After the High Queen and her armies had come, they had breached the barrier around Earth's umbra, allowing far more magic into the world.

It was a lot like shooting, really. I needed the same kind of discipline and mental focus to summon and direct the power. I learned basic spells to cloud the minds of others, to make them more favorably disposed to me. I learned to wrap myself in illusion, to disguise myself using a spell of Masking.

But the most powerful spell I learned was the Cloak.

With the Cloak spell, I could make myself completely invisible, undetectable by the senses or any magical spell. It did have a severe limitation, though – the minute I moved, the spell ended and I would be visible once more. Nevertheless, it was a powerful spell, and I surprised Morvilind by learning in quickly. In time, he told me, I could develop enough skill that I could Cloak myself while I moved, though that would take years of practice.

The thought thrilled me. I dreamed of having that much power. I wanted enough power that I could cure Russell. I also wanted enough power that I could break free of Morvilind's tyranny.

Because at the age of fifteen, after nearly ten years of nonstop training and study and work, I understood what Morvilind wanted of me.

He wanted me to steal things for him.

The first job was a bank in Minneapolis. I think it was a test of sort. Using the skills and magic that Morvilind and his retainers had taught me, I accessed the bank, overrode its security systems, stole an ancient golden necklace from a safe deposit box, and escaped without anyone even realizing that a theft had taken place.

Morvilind was pleased.

After that, he began giving me new tasks, each one harder than the first. A statue from a museum in Los Angeles. A rare book from the library of Harvard University. An enchanted ring from the mansion of an Elven noble. A computer hard drive from the offices of an art college in Seattle. Bit by bit I realized why Morvilind had trained me.

Morvilind was greedy. He liked antiquities and art, both from Earth's history and the history of his homeworld, and he didn't want to pay for them. So he had trained me as an expert thief. He could use me to steal anything he wanted, and all the risk fell to me. If I screwed up, if I was captured, no one would believe the word of a human thief over an Elven noble archmage.

Or Morvilind could just use that vial of heart's blood to kill me.

And if I was killed, Russell would die.

So I didn't screw up. I pushed myself hard, and I was careful. I had some close calls, but I always got away clean.

When I turned eighteen, Morvilind let me get my own apartment. So long as he had that vial of my blood, he could find me anywhere, kill me anywhere, summon me from anywhere. I asked if I could do some jobs on the side, and he answered that it was no concern of his if I got myself killed and let Russell die of frostfever.

I started stealing for myself, squirreling away the money. I tried to seek out magical texts, volumes that could increase my power and magical skill.

I wanted power. I wanted freedom. I wanted to be so powerful that no one could ever hurt me or Russell again.

Or, at the very least, I wanted to be free of Morvilind.

I would find a way.

Somehow.

###

A few days after my twentieth birthday, I felt the summons from Morvilind.

I was in my apartment. I lived in the basement apartment of an old house in Wauwatosa, one of the suburbs of Milwaukee. My landlord thought I was a student at the nearby medical college. At least, that was what all my paperwork and electronic records said. So long as the rent cleared, I don't think he cared.

Specifically, when the summons came, I was hanging from my pull-up bar, working through my second set, sweat drenching my workout shirt and shorts. The magical summons rolled through me in a wave of pain, my muscles going rigid. I caught myself before I hit the floor, and a jolt of pain went through my elbows and shoulders. I let go of the bar, hit the floor with a grunt, and lay down for moment, waiting until my head stopped spinning before I got up again. Morvilind's magical summons always felt like a kick to the gut.

At least it hadn't happened in the middle of a job this time.

I couldn't ignore it. If I delayed too much, he would just keep casting the spell, first daily, then hourly, until I obeyed and came to his mansion in Shorewood.

Best to find out what he wanted from me.

I took a deep breath and went to get ready. My basement apartment had only one bedroom, but since I never had guests, I had converted the living room and the dining room into a small gym and a workshop, with weights, a treadmill, a computer, and a workbench for my various tools. The bedroom held my other equipment, my clothes, my cosmetics, and most of my bookshelves. My bed was also tucked in there someplace.

I showered off and dressed in jeans, a black tank top, and sneakers, and tied my hair back into a tail. There was no point in taking any weapons or equipment except for two of my phones. If I brought weapons, at best Morvilind would be amused. At worst, he would be offended and decide to punish me. It was June, which in Wisconsin meant it could get up to ninety degrees Fahrenheit, but I snatched a heavy leather jacket and a helmet with a visor as I left my apartment.

I needed them for my bike.

Motorcycles are an impractical vehicle in the Midwest for about a third of the year, but I loved them nonetheless. I loved the speed of them, I loved the power, and the minute I had stolen enough money to afford one, I had gone out and bought a Royal Engines NX-9 motorcycle with a six cylinder engine and a black body with orange highlights. Technically, the dealer called it a "sport bike", but I didn't care. It was fast, and when riding it I felt…

Free, I suppose. I knew it was only an illusion. But the illusion was fun while it lasted.

Maybe someday I would have the kind of power for real.

I went to the ramshackle shed that served as my apartment building's shared garage, started my bike, and headed into traffic. Milwaukee was a big city, with nearly two million people spread out along Lake Michigan. It had once been smaller, or so I'd read, but Chicago had been destroyed during the Conquest.

I wondered if traffic had been as bad before the Conquest.

Eventually I worked my way north of the city proper, putting on speed. About an hour's ride brought me to Morvilind's estate. I rode through the gates of the grounds and up the long driveway to his mansion. When I had first seen it as a child fifteen years ago, I had thought it looked like a vast pile of glass and marble. Now I thought the Elven style of architecture looked like a peculiar mixture of Imperial Chinese and old Roman designs, with ornamentations on the side that seemed vaguely Celtic but were in fact Elven hieroglyphics. (Evidently the Elves had their own alphabet for day-to-day use, but used hieroglyphs for formal documents and for spell work.) I parked my bike in front of the mansion's grand doors of red wood, placing my helmet on the seat and draping my jacket over the handlebars. I didn't worry about someone stealing it. No one would dare to steal from an Elven lord.

Well. No one except me.

Morvilind's butler awaited me at the door, a paunchy middle-aged man named Rusk. He wore the formal garb of a household servant, a long red coat and black trousers, the sleeves adorned with black scrollwork, a golden badge of rank upon his high collar. Even the phone at his belt was in a red and black case.

"Miss Moran," rumbled Rusk. He did not approve of me. I didn't know how much he knew about his master's business, but he did not like me and considered me a necessary evil in his domain. "Lord Morvilind awaits you in the library. I shall take you there at once."

I grinned at him. "No need, Mr. Rusk." I patted him on the shoulder, and he cringed away as if my hand had been covered in poison. "I know the way. I've been here before. Or did you forget? You should really get that checked out. Memory loss is a bad symptom in an older gentleman like yourself."

I may have mentioned before that I have a smart mouth.

"If you will accompany me, Miss Moran," rumbled Rusk, but I was already walking past him. I heard the butler sigh as he followed me into the depths of Morvilind's mansion.

Like most Elven architecture, it was light and airy, with lots of open space and red-painted walls, the wooden floor polished to a mirror sheen. Morvilind had a taste for the art of ancient Earth, and so Roman and Egyptian and Greek statues stood in niches or upon plinths. Morvilind had also listened to the advice of the experts who had trained me in various illegal skills, and my practiced eye noticed the signs of expensive security systems, small cameras and infrared lasers and pressure plates. I would not have wanted to rob this place, not even with the aid magic.

Morvilind's library occupied a large room at the rear of the house, high windows overlooking the bluffs and the endlessly churning waters of Lake Michigan. The floor was white marble, polished and gleaming. Books written in both high Elven hieroglyphics and the common Elven alphabet covered the walls, along with countless volumes on ancient Earth's history and peoples. An elaborate summoning circle had been carved into slabs of gleaming red marble before the high windows, a design so intricate that my eye could not follow it. I recognized maybe a quarter of the glyphs and symbols and runes in the design. Long tables ran the length of the room, holding books and scrolls and relics. One table held the tools and instruments a wizard needed to create alchemical potions, essentially spells in a bottle. Before the summoning circle itself stood a high table covered with computer equipment, complete with three enormous monitors arrayed in a semicircle.

Lord Morvilind stood at the table, watching the computer displays. As ever, he wore his black robe with gold trim and the red cloak of an Elven noble. I don't think I had never seen him wear anything else. The monitor on the left showed a strange language I didn't recognize. The central monitor scrolled through three different windows of text, while the one on the right displayed what looked like news footage of a party.

"My lord Morvilind," said Rusk. "Miss Nadia Moran to see you."

"Thank you, Rusk," said Morvilind in his deep, rasping voice. "You may go."

Rusk bowed and strode from the library, and I went to one knee and bowed my head.

"Lord Morvilind," I said, keeping my eyes on the gleaming marble floor. For once, I did not make any smart remarks. Morvilind never grew angry if I did. I don't think I had ever seen him lose his temper. Instead, he simply lifted the crystal vial holding my heart's blood and inflicted a wave of excruciating pain on me. While I writhed on the floor, he waited patiently and resumed his instructions once I was coherent again.

Like he was training me. Like I was his damned dog.

The thought filled my throat with bile, but I kept the anger from my expression.

"Rise, Miss Moran," said Morvilind at last, turning to face me. I rose, and he regarded me with those ancient, icy blue eyes. "I trust you have kept yourself in training?"

"Yes, my lord," I said.

His thin lip twitched in something that was almost a contemptuous smile. "Given the expense of that motorcycle you rolled up my driveway, it seems you have kept yourself profitably occupied indeed."

"It allows me to answer your summons all the quicker, my lord," I said.

He stared at me without blinking, and I saw him turning something over in the fingers of his right hand. It was the crystal vial holding the blood from my heart. A little flicker of fear went through me. With it, he could use his magic to do almost anything he wanted to me. If he decided that my last remark had been impudent, he could use the vial to fill me with unbearable agony.

It was cold in the library, thanks to the air conditioning, but a drop of sweat slithered between my shoulders anyway.

I may not have been his dog, but he did not need anything as crude as a leash to control me. Between the blood and Russell, he could make me do anything he wanted.

How I hated it.

"Answer a question," said Morvilind, turning and tapping a sequence on a keyboard. The monitor on the right shifted to display the face of a middle-aged white man in an expensive-looking suit. He was handsome in a bloodless sort of way, clean-shaven with graying hair and rimless glasses. "Do you know this man?"

"No." I hesitated. "But…I know him from somewhere."

"When was the last time you ate a McCade Foods canned meat product?" said Morvilind.

I almost wrinkled up my nose in disgust. "The canned meat all the veterans like? Never."

"Why not?" said Morvilind.

"Because...it's full of salt and chemicals and grease," I said. "If I wanted high blood pressure and morbid obesity, I would at least have a bacon cheeseburger and enjoy the taste…ah, my lord."

Morvilind did not care. Likely he considered the culinary needs of humans beneath his notice.

"This man's name is Paul McCade," said Morvilind. "His father John was a man-at-arms in the army of the Duke of Sioux Falls, and served with distinction in the battles against the Archons across the Warded Ways of the Shadowlands. After the elder McCade retired from the Duke's service, he took his retirement pay as a pig farm in South Dakota. John McCade proved to have a talent for business, and by the time of his death, McCade Foods was the biggest producer of meat in North America, and McCade himself one of the richest humans in the United Sates. After he died, Paul inherited the company." A look of amused contempt went over Morvilind's face. "Unlike his father, who was proud to think of himself as a working-class man who had done well, Paul views himself as a member of the elite. Consequently, he makes certain to ape the tastes of his betters."

"A lot of imitation Elven art and architecture?" I said before I could stop myself.

"Correct," said Morvilind. "Gaudy and tasteless. However, like his betters, Paul McCade collects ancient human artwork. Specifically, he has a taste for ancient Assyrian artifacts, taken from eastern Asia before the Caliphate destroyed most of them."

"And I suppose," I said, "you want me to get one of those artifacts?"

"You suppose correctly," said Morvilind. "A stone tablet, weighing approximately nine pounds." He tapped some keys, and the image on the right monitor changed from Paul McCade's smug face to a tablet of gray stone covered with strange, angular writing. I didn't recognize it, but it did look the same as the symbols upon the left monitor.

"What is it?" I said.

"A tablet," said Morvilind, "containing a passage from a certain text. I wish to add it to my collection."

I shrugged. "It's right there. If you know the language the computer can translate it for you."

"I require the tablet itself," said Morvilind. "You will obtain it for me."

I looked at the tablet, at Morvilind, and then back at the tablet.

"It's magical, isn't it?" I said. "That's why you want me to steal it. If you just needed to translate the text, you could do it here. The tablet itself must be enchanted."

"You reason correctly," said Morvilind.

I let out a long breath and stared at the image of the tablet.

"Is McCade a Rebel?" I said.

"Not to my knowledge," said Morvilind.

That was not a reassuring answer. The High Queen might have ruled over Earth for three centuries, but not everyone was satisfied with her rule. The news didn't report on it, but there were underground Rebel groups. Sometimes they were little more than disgruntled thugs. Sometimes they were well-armed terrorists. And sometimes they tapped into forbidden magic in an effort to overthrow the High Queen. I didn't care about the Rebels or their stupid plans, but I had gotten caught in the crossfire between the Inquisition and the Rebels during a previous job, and I didn't want to repeat the experience.

"You have to tell me if he's a Rebel," I said. Morvilind gave me a cold look. "My lord. If he's a Rebel, and the Inquisition comes for him and I get caught…"

"There is no danger to me," said Morvilind, raising the crystal vial. "I can kill you from a distance long before you reveal anything harmful to me."

Well. That was reassuring.

"But if I'm captured or killed," I said, "you'll never get the tablet." He made no reaction to that. "And you'd have to waste ten or fifteen years training my replacement."

Morvilind remained silent, but he tapped the crystal vial with a finger. I flinched, expecting him to send a wave of pain at me through the link of the heart's blood, but nothing happened. He was playing with me, and likely enjoyed the reaction. I was furious at myself for the show of weakness, and I forced myself to remain motionless, to wait for his answer.

"I do not believe that he is a Rebel," said Morvilind at last. "He is too rich to be the poorer sort of Rebel, and not philosophical enough to be the richer kind of Rebel. Nevertheless, you have deduced at least part of the truth. McCade has an unhealthy interest in magic, especially for a man who was never part of the Wizards' Legion. So he collects magical artifacts in secret. Most of his trinkets are useless, but the tablet…I want the tablet. So you are going to get it for me, and you shall obtain it for me within a month."

"A month?" I said. "It will be hard to pull a job like that off in a month."

"A month," repeated Morvilind. "Do not disappoint me, Nadia Moran. It would be tragic if your brother succumbed at last to frostfever after so many years of treatment."

"I can't do it in a month," I said. Morvilind gave the crystal vial a tap, but I kept talking. "McCade is a billionaire, and he'll have the kind of security money like that can buy. I can get through it, but I need time to prepare. A couple of months, minimum."

"As it happens, you shall soon have an excellent opportunity," said Morvilind. "McCade will host a Conquest Day gala in honor of the Duke of Milwaukee, and Lord Tamirlas and his chief vassals shall graciously make an appearance."

"They'll have their own security," I said, dubious. "Maybe even a few Inquisitors." Yet I saw the potential in the idea. Hundreds of guests would descend upon McCade's mansion for the gala. Even if they brought their own bodyguards, that many guests would strain McCade's security resources. It might be possible to walk off with the tablet during the gala.

Maybe. Maybe not.

"I see the wheels turning," said Morvilind. "You shall come up with a plan, I have no doubt. The gala is in three weeks."

"Three weeks?" I said.

"Conquest Day, at least in the United States, is on July 4th."

"I can't do it that quickly."

Morvilind stared at me, his pale, blue-tinged lips twitching into a smile. He was enjoying this, the bastard. "I believe one of your race's own philosophers said that a hanging is a marvelous way of focusing the mind. Consider your brother, consider the death that awaits him from untreated frostfever, contemplate that deeply…and I believe inspiration shall simply leap into your mind." He turned from me, facing his monitors once again. "You may go. Rusk shall see you out. Return here once you have the tablet."

I stared at his back for a moment, shaking with anger.

"My lord," I ground out. He would punish me if I didn't say it.

Morvilind waved a hand in dismissal, and I strode out of the library. Rusk waited to escort me from the mansion, but I blew past him, stalked past the ancient statues and the Elven hieroglyphics, and out the door and back to my bike. I tugged on my helmet and threw on my jacket, pausing to check my bike's handlebars.

The pause was also to make my hands stop shaking.

Three weeks. Three weeks to figure out how to steal something from one of the most heavily guarded buildings in Milwaukee.

I took deep breaths, focusing something other than the anger and the fear. The magical lessons and the unarmed combat training I had received had one other benefit. They allowed me to focus my mind quickly, to calm myself and come up with a plan.

So, a plan.

One thing to do first.

I reached into my coat pocket, drew out a cheap phone, and sent a text message. I dropped the phone back into my pocket, bit my lip for a moment, and nodded to myself.

I started up my motorcycle and left Morvilind's mansion behind, heading south. Tomorrow, I would come up with a plan. Tonight, I would see the reason I was doing all of this.

Tonight, I was going to go see my baby brother.

CHAPTER 2
FAMILY

The air smelled of barbecue as I turned the corner from 76th Street to Wisconsin Avenue. I rode past row after row of little two-story, three bedroom houses with fenced yards and narrow driveways. Many of the men-at-arms of the Duke of Milwaukee and his vassals settled here after they received their retirement pay, so I saw a lot of stern-looking middle-aged guys wearing T-shirts adorned with the Elven hieroglyphics of the lords they had served. I saw veterans with shirts bearing the hieroglyphs of Duke Tamirlas of Milwaukee, or the Barons of Wauwatosa and Brookfield and Brown Deer, the Knights of Granville and the Third Ward.

Many of the veterans were missing fingers or arms or legs. I saw a lot of wheelchairs and crutches, and many more women than men. Many men came back wounded from the wars in the Shadowlands, but many men never came back at all.

At least I would never have to worry about that for Russell.

I came to a nice little house on a tree-shaded street. It had a small front yard with a well-tended garden, and a flagpole over the front door flew the colors of the High Queen, the United States, and the House of Morvilind. A little wooden mailbox (hand-crafted, of course) said MARNEYS on the side. I rolled my bike to the curb, put down the kickstand, and hopped off. The garage door was closed, the curtains drawn. I wondered where Dr. Marney and his wife had gone. I pulled my main phone out and glanced at the time.

12:42 PM on a Sunday. Then I felt like an idiot.

They had gone to church.

I wasn't sure how I felt about the Marneys taking Russell to church with them. I wanted Russell to grow up knowing right from wrong. Which was odd, coming from a professional thief, but I wanted Russell to have a good life, a normal life, a happy life.

Which meant a life away from Elves and their politics…and away from people like me.

But I disliked the idea of church. More to the point, I disliked the idea of God. It wasn't that I didn't believe in God, more that I thought Him incompetent, or maybe a fraud. Like, God was supposed to be good, so why had my parents died? Why was Russell afflicted with frostfever? Why was I forced to undertake dangerous and illegal tasks for Morvilind?

The worst part was that Russell and I had it comparatively good. Or better than a lot of people. Russell wasn't fighting the Archons and God knows what other horrors in the Shadowlands. I wasn't technically a slave, and I did not spend my days scrubbing an Elven lord's floor or warming the bed of an Elven lord perverted enough to like human women.

For that matter, we were both still alive.

I had driven past the spell-haunted ruins of Chicago and Baltimore enough times to know what happened to those who provoked the High Queen. Which in turn made me angry when I thought of God again. If He was supposed to be good, why did things like that happen?

The Marneys came home while I stood brooding next to my motorcycle.

So much for the uncanny senses of a master thief.

Dr. James Marney drove an old Duluth Car Company sedan with a few dents in the side. It was an unfortunate shade of brown, but James was too frugal to buy a car with a better color. Given that his frugality helped him keep a roof over Russell's head, I couldn't complain. The car rolled up to the garage, and I followed it. The doors swung open, and James got out, hobbling a bit until he could get his cane out. He was a tall, bony man with a graying crew-cut and a lined face. His wife Lucy came out of the passenger side, still athletic and trim despite her age. The back door of the car opened…

"Nadia!"

Russell flew across the driveway and caught me in a hug.

It had only been five weeks since I had seen him last, but I swear he had grown six inches since then. He was only fourteen, but he was already taller than I was, which simply did not seem fair. Our father had been tall, I remembered that much about him. By the time Russell finished growing, I would have to crane my neck to look up at him.

He was thinner than he should have been at his age, his face gaunt and angular. His hair and eyebrows were a ghostly shade of white, a side effect of the frostfever that boiled in his veins. Morvilind's magic had contained the disease, keeping it from killing him or spreading to anyone else, but the illness still exacted a physical cost on him.

At least that meant he couldn't be conscripted into the High Queen's armies the way that Dr. Marney had been, the way my father's magical ability had taken him into the Wizards' Legion.

I kept all those musings from my expression. I didn't get to see Russell as often as I liked, so I tried to keep these visits positive. I wanted him to have a good life, a happy life.

A life that wasn't anything at all like the way mine would likely end.

So I slipped out of his hug and grinned up at him.

"You," I said, "have gotten taller." I tapped his chin. "And you're going to have to start shaving soon."

Russell grimaced at that. "I have, once. I didn't like it. It felt like peeling my face."

"You get used to it, son," said James, limping over. He could walk, but his right leg remained rigid, and most of his weight went upon his cane. Years ago, while serving in Morvilind's men-at-arms in the Shadowlands, James had taken an orcish axe to the leg. He hadn't lost the leg, and he hadn't died of infection or gangrene, but his dancing days were done. After taking his pension, James went into civilian medical practice and married one of the nurses. Lucy couldn't have children for some reason or another, and so they adopted.

Specifically, they adopted Russell. Lord Morvilind, in his great concern for the veterans who had served as his men-at-arms, had arranged for James and Lucy to adopt a poor orphan boy from the kindness of his generous heart…

"Nadia?" said Russell.

Some of my sour thoughts must have reflected on my face.

"Stiff back," I said. "Too long on the bike."

"Those things will kill you," said Lucy. From another woman, the remark might have been condescending. From her, the concern was genuine. She had been a nurse for a long time.

"I always ride carefully," I lied. Honestly, I sometimes thought a motorcycle crash might be a better fate than what awaited me if I kept doing Morvilind's work. But if that happened before Morvilind finished casting the spell to cure frostfever, Russell would die.

Six more years. I just had to hang on for another six years. And then…well, then I would figure something out.

"What brings you over?" said James, gesturing towards the house's back door. We walked there in a slow group, in deference to James's bad leg. "I thought you'd be busy."

"Lord Morvilind has a job for me," I said. James and Lucy and Russell didn't know what I really did. They thought I was a computer programmer, and I knew just enough about computers to maintain the illusion. Russell was pretty clever, and if he got interested enough in computers that lie was going to come back to haunt me someday. "It's going to take a couple of weeks, and I don't know when I'll be back."

Russell looked anxious. "It's not dangerous, is it?"

"Nope," I said. "Just sitting at a desk and pressing buttons. The only danger is that I'll die of boredom."

"Lord Morvilind must have great trust in you," said Lucy, unlocking the door.

I laughed. "I wish he would find someone else to trust. His lordship can be pretty demanding at…"

"Don't be elfophobic, dear," said Lucy as she stepped into the kitchen.

That was the other thing that bothered me about the Marneys. Though to be fair, it bothered me about most people.

They…revered the Elves. Respected them. I had spent too much time around Morvilind to think that way. I knew the Elves regarded humans as loyal dogs at best and cattle at worst. But the Marneys had been raised to revere the Elves, and even James with his experience of the Shadowlands still respected Morvilind.

They were teaching Russell to revere the Elves.

I don't know why it bothered me. It shouldn't have bothered me. Russell had a good home, and if things went well he would have a good life once he was cured of frostfever. I wasn't a Rebel, to dream of liberating mankind from the Elves. I wanted Russell to have a good life…and I wanted to have enough power that no one could ever have a hold over me the way that Morvilind did.

So it shouldn't matter what the Marneys and Russell thought of the Elves, but it still annoyed me.

"You're right," I said. I didn't want to fight. "I'm sorry. Russell, how's school?"

He brightened up at that. Russell liked school. I worried that his inability to join athletics and his intellectual interests would turn the other kids against him, but he had the rare gift of pursuing his interests without giving a damn about the opinions of his peers. Paradoxically, that seemed to make him popular. Teenagers are weird. James encouraging him towards medical school, though Russell's natural interests were toward computer science. Yet he took to biology well. If he could get his head around the math requirement, he might have a good career as a doctor. God knew the United States wasn't about to run out of sick people…and plenty of wounded veterans returned from the High Queen's campaigns in the Shadowlands.

He might have a life that was nothing like mine.

We spent most of the afternoon talking. Russell told me about his classes and his friends. Apparently he had joined an automotive club, and spent some of his afternoons taking apart cars and rebuilding them. I approved, though I was careful not to show too much approval. Car repair was a practical skill, and if any of his other career choices didn't work out, it might give him a good living away from the notice of the Elven nobles. I told some highly edited versions of my work for Morvilind that contained maybe five percent of the truth. James managed to work in a few invitations to his church, and Lucy asked in skillfully indirect ways when I was going to find a husband and start having children, and mentioned that their church had a plethora of eligible bachelors of quality character.

I didn't mind the questions about my marital status. If the Marneys didn't care about me, they wouldn't ask the questions. Though I certainly couldn't tell them the truth that I did not want a husband or even a lover. Morvilind held too much power over me already. If gave my heart to someone, he would have power over me, and there was no way I would ever voluntarily surrender that much power.

Not again. Not after the disaster of the one time I had fallen in love. I didn't want to dwell on that, though, so I steered the conversation towards food.

Eventually, I helped Lucy make dinner, while James and Russell went onto the tiny back porch to grill steaks while Lucy and I made salad.

"Steak and leafy green vegetables," said Lucy, washing a cucumber and passing it to me. I started slicing it up. "Just like you prefer."

"Thank you," I said. "Protein and vegetables are the healthiest. And you didn't have to go to all this trouble for me, you know."

Lucy laughed. "What trouble? I'm making you chop the vegetables. I hate that part."

"Fair enough." I swept the cucumbers into the bowl.

"For a computer programmer," said Lucy, washing some more vegetables, "you're in very good shape."

I shrugged. "I exercise a lot."

"I help with physical therapy at the hospital," said Lucy. "Missing limbs from the battles in the Shadowlands, that kind of thing." Her eyes strayed to the window over the sink. James stood at the grill, cane in one hand, and spatula in the other. "So I know the average fitness level of a woman your age…and you are way beyond that."

I shrugged again. "Like I said, I exercise a lot. I spend all day sitting at a computer, so the exercise is to make up for that." I swept some more cucumbers into the bowl, hoping she would change the subject.

"The…work you do for Lord Morvilind," said Lucy, looking into the sink. "Is it ever…dangerous?"

I said nothing for a moment, watching as Russell started to flip the steaks on the grill.

"Life is dangerous," I said at last.

"Be careful," said Lucy. "Please. For Russell's sake. You're all the family he has left."

"You're his parents," I said. "He doesn't even remember our mom and dad. You've been there for him far more than I have."

"You're his sister," said Lucy. "If he lost you, I don't think he could handle it." She swallowed. "We'd be upset, too. James and I. You can stay here whenever you want, you know."

"Thank you," I said. I never would, though. My "jobs" from Morvilind were far too dangerous. If I made a mistake, if I got arrested by Homeland Security or, God forbid, the Inquisition, and if the Marneys and Russell were with me when I was arrested…

No. I would have be careful. That meant not staying here.

"Well," I said. "Do you want to talk about our feelings some more, or should I crack some eggs for the salad?"

Lucy laughed at that. "So that is where Russell gets that smart mouth from." She opened the refrigerator and handed me a carton of eggs.

By the time we finished the salad, Russell and James returned with the steaks, and we withdrew to the dining room. Like the rest of the house, it was small but cozy. On one wall was a cross and a picture of Jesus with some sheep. On the other wall was a portrait of the High Queen Tarlia, stern and regal in her silvery armor, with a banner bearing Morvilind's hieroglyphs hanging from the frame. I'd asked Morvilind once why the High Queen had not crushed the churches the way she had destroyed so many other organizations and factions during the Conquest.

To my surprise, he had answered me.

"Give to Caesar what is Caesar's and to God what is God's, is that not the traditional doctrine of the western churches?" Morvilind had said. "Those who can accept the High Queen as their Caesar…well, Her Majesty is a pragmatic woman, and she will leave them in peace so long as they serve her. For those who do not accept her as their Caesar, you can drive past the ruins of Chicago to see what Her Majesty does when pragmatism fails."

I shuddered a little as I passed the High Queen's portrait, but fortunately no one noticed. James and Lucy and millions of others had no trouble accepting such an arrangement. Me, I didn't care. I was no Rebel. I just wanted Russell to be safe and happy.

And enough power to make sure no one like Morvilind could ever dominate me again.

James said grace, which in the Marney household was an affair of five minutes, asking God to bless everyone he knew, and asking Him to grant wisdom to Lord Morvilind, Duke Tamirlas, and the High Queen. I squirmed at that part, but thankfully everyone else had their eyes closed.

The meal was delicious. James knew how to grill a good steak, and he had passed that skill to Russell. For a while we sat in silence, too preoccupied with the food. Later the conversation turned to its previous easy rhythm, with James and Lucy telling me about their work at the hospital. After dinner I helped clear the table, while Russell loaded the dishwasher. I wandered back into the living room, opened the closet, and checked in the pocket of my coat. I had my main phone in my jeans pocket, of course, but in my line of work I went through a lot of burner phones, and one of them was in my coat. I had a new text message, an answer to the one I had sent from that phone earlier.

It said that I had an appointment at 10:00 AM in exactly eight days.

Eight days. I thought through the implications. Would eight days be enough? It ought to be. I would have to start tonight, and…

"Nadia?"

I blinked, tucked the burner phone back into my jacket, and turned as James hobbled into the living room.

"Leaving yet?" he said, holding a small white package the size of a deck of cards. "I wouldn't what you to miss out."

I glanced over my shoulder, saw Lucy and Russell busy in the kitchen. "You're a saint."

"No, I'm not. Come on," said James, leaning on his cane. "We should probably talk."

I sighed. "Right." I followed him onto the front step. June days in Wisconsin last a long time, but the sun was fading away to the west. James sat down with a grunt on the concrete step, the cane propped against one of Lucy's potted flower bushes. I sat down next to him, and James opened the little pack of cigarettes. Some restricted items are available only to veterans who have honorably completed their term of service in the Shadowlands under an Elven lord, and cigarettes were one of them. Naturally, there was a black market, but I never bought them. Cigarettes were expensive, and I didn't have the money to waste. And I didn't want to use anything that might make me weaker.

Nonetheless, I really enjoyed cigarettes.

"Those things will kill you," I said as he passed me one.

James grunted. "I'm fifty-five. Something's going to kill me eventually. The Lord will take me in his own good time." He lit his cigarette with a lighter, and I lit mine off the end of his. We sat in silence for a moment, puffing. The smoke burned a little going in, but left a warm, pleasant feeling in my chest. Of course, too much of it would leave my lungs a scarred ruin.

"You tell Lucy about these?" I said.

James smiled. "I love my wife, but I don't tell her everything. You love Russell. But you don't tell him everything, do you?"

I stared into the gathering twilight, watching the smoke rise from the end of the cigarette. "No. So why smoke with me?"

"You're not a veteran," said James.

"Of course not," I said. "The High Queen only wants men for her armies. Women can stay home and make the next generation of soldiers."

"You're not a veteran," said James, "but you know some things that only men who have served as men-at-arms should know. It sometimes turns up in the things you say. You know how guns work. You know a lot about magic. And the Shadowlands…"

I felt a chill. "What about the Shadowlands?"

"You can always tell," said James, "when someone has seen the Shadowlands."

I thought of that strange, terrible place between the worlds, a place where guns and electronics did not work, where men had to fight with swords and spears and arrows as their ancestors had. I thought of some of the creatures I had seen, things that gave me nightmares still.

"I suppose you can," I said.

"So whatever work Lord Morvilind has you doing," said James, "I'd wager it's more dangerous than computer programming."

"You know I can't talk about it," I said.

"No," said James. "And I trust Lord Morvilind's wisdom." It took some effort, but I didn't laugh. The last thing I wanted was another lecture about elfophobia. "But there are so many strange things about you. When we took Russell in, I thought Lord Morvilind would place both of you in our house. Yet he let Russell live with us, and you stayed to work for him."

I said nothing. What could I say? That Morvilind used me to break the law and steal things for him? That I knew magic and spells that humans were forbidden to learn, that the Inquisition would execute me if they ever found out? That Morvilind had a vial of my heart's blood and I didn't dare to disobey him, to say nothing of what would happen to Russell?

"The only thing that matters," I said, "is that I love Russell, and I want what is best for him. And I'm grateful to you for taking care of him for all these years."

James sighed. "I suppose you have an envelope for me?"

"Left it on your desk," I said. "If I'm not back by two weeks after Conquest Day, open it up. I've got some money set aside. The documents in the envelope can help you find it. It can help Russell. Maybe you can find another Elven wizard willing to work on the frostfever cure. Because if I don't come back, Lord Morvilind won't help Russell."

"Your work for Lord Morvilind," said James, "is that dangerous?"

"Extremely," I said, thinking of my limited time frame. "More so than usual, for this job." I put out the cigarette and stood up. "I should go. It's time to get to work."

James got to his feet with a grunt, leaning on his cane. "Be careful, Nadia. We shall pray for you."

I started to say that if God really cared what happened to people, then my parents would still be alive, but I stopped myself. James didn't deserve that...and I needed all the help I could get. "Thank you."

I went back inside, retrieved my jacket and helmet, and said my goodbyes. I took one last look at Russell, realizing it might be the last time I ever saw him.

Then I got on my motorcycle and drove into the darkness.

It was time to get to work.

CHAPTER 3
PREPARATIONS

I had eight days before my appointment, and I put them to good use.

Using the Internet for anything in my line of work is dangerous. Morvilind's teachers had told me that the last few pre-Conquest Presidents had built huge computer systems to monitor the Internet, both to spy on the various groups that eventually became the Caliphate and to monitor their own political opponents. After the Conquest, the Inquisition had taken over those computer systems and maintained them to this day.

So I had to be very, very careful.

Not that I did anything stupid. Going on a social network and complaining about the High Queen or one of the nobles would lead to a Homeland Security squad kicking down your door, followed by a public flogging (broadcast live on the Internet) on Punishment Day, a steep fine, and status as a lifelong pariah. But there were subtler dangers. If, for example, someone robbed Paul McCade, and investigators realized that I had been doing a lot of searches about him before the robbery, they might start sniffing around me.

That would be bad.

I was careful. There were ways to avoid the Inquisition's online eye, and Morvilind's teachers had taught them to me, a maze of hardware scramblers and false accounts and redirected connections. It helped that most of what I wanted to know was public information, available on various government sites and job boards. In a short time I had McCade's home address, his official biography, and the names of the companies he hired to clean his palatial mansion and to cater the lavish parties he hosted.

Specifically, the name of the catering company he had hired to provide food for his Conquest Day gala.

I got jobs at both companies. That part wasn't hard. Service companies tended to hire unmarried women and married women whose husbands were serving as men-at-arms in one Elven noble's army or another, so they had a lot of employee turnover. I forged the necessary credentials and forms, and Natalia Smith joined the Duncan Catering Company, and Jesse Clarke got hired by the EZClean Cleaners. I spent a couple of days at both jobs, going through employee orientation and helping the cleaners vacuum mansions along the lake shore and the caterers prepare shrimp plates and truffles for various fancy parties. I kept my head down, didn't ask a lot of questions, but made sure that I got my work done ahead of schedule and without any complaints.

That endeared me to my supervisors (my fellow employees did not tend to be the most competent or motivated), so I had no trouble getting assigned to the EZClean crew scheduled to clean McCade's mansion before the party, or to the Duncan Catering Company team that would cater McCade's Conquest Day gala. I felt bad about that the deceptions, but if my plan worked, no suspicion would fall upon either company. And if it didn't work…well, if I had to choose between Russell and a bunch of strangers, Russell would win every single time.

Two days before my appointment, I drove downtown to take a look at Paul McCade's mansion.

I didn't take my motorcycle. A Royal Engines NX-9 motorcycle wasn't the most expensive bike available, but it was not the sort of vehicle a woman like Natalia Smith or Jesse Clarke would drive. Instead I stopped by my rented storage unit and got one of the cars I had purchased under a false name, a fifteen year old green Duluth Car Company sedan with a hundred and fifty thousand miles, dents along the right side, and an air conditioning system that sounded like a running food processor. I preferred my motorcycle, but the green sedan was the kind of vehicle that everyone ignored.

Though it did stand out a bit in McCade's neighborhood.

I parked the sedan at one of the public beaches and walked to McCade's mansion. I wore my gray cleaner's coverall, my hair pulled back into a ponytail beneath a baseball cap and a duffel bag over one shoulder, my eyes hidden behind sunglasses and a wireless earpiece in my right ear. To anyone who looked, I would seem to be a janitor going to work.

So I was able to take a good, long look at Paul McCade's mansion.

It was a big place, set comfortably on a bluff overlooking Lake Michigan, surrounded by acres of close-cropped green grass. The mansion itself was a five-story monstrosity, built in the same Elven style as Morvilind's mansion, but McCade's mansion simply looked gaudy. I didn't think he had intended his mansion to scream "I have too much damn money", but it shouted the message so loudly I almost needed earplugs.

The front courtyard had been enclosed in glass beneath an elaborate skylight, the space large enough to comfortably hold hundreds of people. I saw tables and chairs within it. McCade's gala would take place there, and then in the gallery in the mansion proper.

The tablet that Morvilind wanted might well be within that gallery. I had found an article about McCade's art collection in the sort of gushy lifestyle magazine that got really excited about hardwood floors. McCade displayed many of his prize pieces in the gallery beyond the glassed-in courtyard. He had a secure vault deeper in the mansion that held some of the more valuable objects, and I was certain that he had security measures that he had neglected to mention to the magazine, and perhaps had failed to mention to Homeland Security.

I walked slowly past the mansion, crossed the street, and circled past it again. My earpiece included a handy little camera, dumping a video recording to my phone. That night I returned to my apartment, copied the footage to my computer's hard drive and reviewed it carefully, taking note of the location of cameras and floodlights and motion sensors. Then I went for an early morning shift at the catering company, helping to prepare several orders of pastries for the company's clients. The cooks were grateful for the help.

After that, I hurried to EZClean and joined the crew sent for the weekly cleaning of McCade's mansion. I pulled my hair back into a tight tail, and put a fake ring in my nose, a second in my right eyebrow, and another in each of my ears. I didn't have any real piercings – they were too much of a liability in a fight – but they did a marvelous job of changing my appearance when necessary. It's amazing how a few bits of jewelry and some makeup can change a face.

We drove a chemical-smelling van to the utility garage of McCade's mansion. A half-dozen bored-looking security men in black suits awaited us, and despite their boredom, they went about their work with competence. They collected our phones, scanned each of us for weapons, and then made us sign the visitor log. Our crew boss then assigned tasks. Mopping the floor in McCade's main art gallery and vacuuming his library were the least popular tasks, since damaging even one of Mr. McCade's exhibits or rare books would result in a lawsuit.

Naturally, I volunteered.

That got me past the courtyard and into the gallery proper, a large hall with a gleaming hardwood floor, various objects of ancient art sitting upon pedestals. I made sure to do a good job of washing and polishing the floor to a mirror sheen while giving the various pieces of Roman, Egyptian, and Assyrian art a wide berth. Alas, the tablet that Morvilind wanted was not in the gallery.

I suppose that would have been too easy.

Once the gallery was done, I headed to the library. Two massive wooden doors opened off from the gallery and led to McCade's library, which was the size of a small town's public library. It had two floors connected by a spiral staircase with a gleaming brass railing, and many smaller rooms opened off the main library, holding rare books. One room had a collection of Mark Twain first editions, while a second held illuminated medieval manuscripts, and a third had a collection of vintage comic books from the 1950s. Glass cases displayed various artifacts and relics, but I saw no trace of the tablet Morvilind wanted.

I did, however, see a massive door like a bank vault on the far side of the library. I pushed the vacuum cleaner closer, rolling it over the thick carpet. A quick glance around confirmed that no one else was in the library. There were three cameras in the ceiling, and at least one of them would see me…but they couldn't detect what I was going to do.

I kept one hand on the vacuum's handle, but I gestured with me free hand, whispering under my breath as I focused my mind and summoned magical power, casting one of the spells that Morvilind had taught me. I worked the spell to sense the presence of magical forces, and I sensed nothing within the library.

But beyond the vault door…

I felt the buzzing, taut presences of several auras of potent magical power.

Well, well, well.

Morvilind was right. McCade liked to collect magical artifacts. An anonymous call to the Inquisition could get McCade into a lot of trouble, and perhaps I could grab the tablet in the chaos. On the other hand, it was likely that the Inquisition already knew about McCade and simply didn't care. McCade's company provided a lot of food for the High Queen's campaigns, and McCade himself was friends with Duke Tamirlas and several other high Elven nobles. A man like him would have privileges that an ordinary subject of the High Queen would not, and if I stole the tablet, the Inquisition and Homeland Security might actually help him get it back.

No. Better to make the tablet disappear without any explanation.

I finished vacuuming the library and rejoined the rest of the crew in the courtyard. We did a quick turndown of McCade's guest rooms, and then trooped back down to the utility garage. The security men checked us over one last time to make sure we hadn't absconded with anything valuable, returned our phones, and bid us good day. We climbed back into the van and drove off. Most of the other workers focused upon their phones, checking their emails and messages, and few others leaned back and went to sleep. I looked out the van's back windows, watching McCade's mansion recede behind us, Lake Michigan like a sheet of rippled gray steel in the distance.

So I saw the man standing on the sidewalk, staring at the van.

He looked unremarkable – white, somewhere between thirty and forty, wearing athletic shoes, old jeans, a baggy hooded sweatshirt, and sunglasses. They were big sunglasses and not a bit stylish, the kind of sunglasses old people wore when they drove into the sun. Because of them, I couldn't get a good look at his face.

But I was certain, absolutely certain, that he was scowling at the van.

That didn't have to mean anything significant. Maybe he had used to work for EZClean Cleaners and had gotten fired. Maybe his ex-girlfriend was in the van. Maybe the van had almost hit him – I had noticed the crew boss sometimes exhibited an alarming indifference to pedestrians.

Or maybe he had noticed me looking around the mansion.

It was unlikely, but in my line of work a little paranoia is a good thing, so I memorized his features as best as I could.

###

My appointment, as it happened, was on Punishment Day.

Punishment Day happened once a week. In pre-Conquest days, criminals had been thrown into hellish prisons for decades, left to torture each other while the guards ignored them or actively participated. The High Queen took a different approach to disciplining her subjects, and the judges at the county, state, and federal levels carried out her will. Minor crimes received fines ranging from light to steep. Moderate crimes received public floggings, from twenty lashes to two hundred, sometimes accompanied by additional fines. Capital crimes were punished by death, whether by hanging or beheading. Those who could not afford their fines were sold into slavery, whether to an Elven noble or to one of the High Queen's work gangs.

Every single punishment was recorded, and on Punishment Day, Homeland Security released the week's videos on the Internet, to inspire the High Queen's subjects to greater virtue by watching the shame of those who had broken the law.

When I got on the bus, most of the other passengers were hunched over their phones, watching this week's crop of punishments. The most popular video this week was of an overweight nineteen-year-old boy from Oregon, the son of a state legislator who had insulted an Elven noble. For the crime of elfophobia, he had been sentenced to sixty lashes. His high-pitched, keening screams as he was tied to the post and flogged to unconsciousness sounded like a terrified little girl, and social media erupted with mockery and derision.

God, but I hated Punishment Day.

I knew I might be the one screaming with terror and agony in one of those videos someday, that I might have even worse in store for me. The thought of being that powerless made my stomach twist…and I didn't have that much power to start. I looked at the other passengers on the bus, some of them laughing and joking as they watched the Punishment Day videos, and for a moment I hated them so much that I could barely keep my bored, sleepy expression in place.

Maybe that's why I wasn't a Rebel. I detested the Elves, but I didn't like humans either.

Well. That, and Morvilind would kill me.

Thankfully, the bus soon reached my stop, and I yanked the yellow cord and got out, leaving the other passengers to their Punishment Day amusements. The bus deposited me near the airport, on a street with a massive rental car dealer on the north side and a row of industrial and office buildings on the south side. I wandered past the office buildings, hands in the pockets of my sweatshirt, my eyes darting back and forth as I watched for pedestrians. No one was on the sidewalks, and only a few cars rumbled up and down the road.

I waited for a gap in the traffic, and then ducked into a windowless alley between two of the office buildings. The alley was deserted, save for a dumpster and a light scattering of trash. I took a deep breath, gathered magical power, and extended my right hand, silver light flashing around my fingers. I held the power for a moment, whispering the words of a spell in the Elven tongue as I focused my will, forcing the power to channel itself into my thoughts. The magic reached a crescendo, and I swept my hand before me, the silver light flaring up and down my body.

The Mask shimmered into existence around me.

The illusion changed my appearance. I stand only five foot three, so the spell made me appear six foot two. It made me look like a man instead of a woman. I had fashioned a Mask in the image of a middle-aged man, balding and slightly paunchy, clad in a white dress shirt, a black sport coat, black trousers, and black dress shoes. Anyone looking at me would see the image of the Mask, not me.

It was a useful spell.

Of course, like all useful things, Masking had limitations. I had to devote at least part of my mind to maintaining the illusion, or it would fall apart or develop obvious inconsistencies. No one would paid attention to a random middle-aged man, but people would notice if his clothes suddenly changed color or random body parts disappeared. It also took a continuous draw of magical power, and I couldn't maintain it forever. Any wizard could detect the Mask easily enough, so it wasn't a spell I could use against another wizard.

Yet when dealing with people who had no magical abilities, a Mask was exceedingly useful. My appointment was with a genius, but he dealt with computers, not spells. I had bought things a couple dozen times from him in the last few years, but he had no idea who I really was, or that I was even a woman. If he was ever arrested, the evidence on his servers would implicate my alias, not me.

I left the alley, strode along the sidewalks, and let myself into one of the office buildings. I headed down the hall until I came to a glass door with NILES RINGER COMPUTER SERVICES stenciled upon it. Beyond was a small waiting room stocked with old magazines and cheap folding chairs, and a bored receptionist playing a computer game involving pieces of fruit.

She looked up at me and managed a false smile. "Yes, sir?"

"Ernie Tesserman to see Mr. Ringer, please," I said. The Mask disguised my voice. I was a soprano, but the Mask gave me the gravelly voice of a fifty-year-old man who had enjoyed a lot of cigarettes. "I should be his ten o'clock."

"He's expecting you," said the receptionist, returning her attention to the fruit on her screen. "Go right in."

I nodded, stepped past the desk, and opened the door.

Niles Ringer's office looked more like a server room, with two rows of steel racks holding rows of humming black boxes covered in blinking green LEDs. Niles himself sat at his desk between the racks, its surface covered with half-assembled computers. He was the fattest man I had ever met, at least three hundred and fifty pounds, and even in the air-conditioned chill he had a faint sheen of sweat on his forehead. He looked harmless at best and ridiculous at worst, but he had been involved in various computer crimes since before I had been born, and he had never been caught. I was also pretty sure he had a variety of weapons hidden under the desk.

Niles looked up from his monitors as I approached, and a smile spread over his face.

"Ah," he said. "Mr. Tesserman. My favorite customer. You always have such unusual requests."

"That's me," I said in my Masked voice. "What about my last request? Can it…"

His phone rang. Niles lifted one thick finger and picked up his phone. I sighed with annoyance, folded my arms over my chest, and waited.

"Yes?" said Niles. "Why, yes, I am? What? No, no. I'm just pretending to talk on my phone." I blinked. "I'm testing my new app." He beamed and rotated his phone's screen to face me. "You see?"

"I don't," I said.

"Well," said Niles, "you know how sometimes you're stuck in an annoying conversation and can't get out of it? With my app, you can set a timer, and it fakes a phone call so you can get out of the conversation."

"Charming." I wondered what Morvilind would do if I tried that with him, and tried not to shudder at the thought. "So I can assume you don't want my business?"

"Of course I want your business," said Niles. "You always pay in cash, and there are never any…complications."

"Complications are like hemorrhoids," I said. "They're bad."

"And I'm familiar with both," said Niles, shifting a bit in his seat.

"That," I said, "was too much information. And not what I paid for."

"You haven't paid me yet," said Niles.

I reached into a pocket of my sweatshirt and drew out an envelope, concentrating on my Mask to make sure it looked like Ernie had reached into the inner pocket of his sport coat. I tossed the envelope on the desk, and Niles drew out the neat little bundle of hundred-dollar bills inside. The High Queen's face gazed out from the bills with aloof serenity.

"You don't have to count it in front of me," I said.

"Trust and openness make for a solid business relationship," said Niles, counting the money. He nodded in satisfaction and then tucked the envelope away in a drawer. He then rummaged within the drawer for a moment, and drew out a small brown envelope.

"You were able to answer my questions?" I said.

"I was," said Niles. "Took a bit of work, but I was able to track down the architectural firm that designed and constructed Paul McCade's mansion. You know, I'm quite fond of McCade's canned meat product. It's really good on a toasted bun with some cheese and mayo."

"That sounds like a heart attack," I said. "And the second thing?"

"A copy of the invitation to his Conquest Day gala?" said Niles. "Got that, too. Or the file template and the holographic watermark, anyway. You'll have to find a high-end printer and print out the invitation yourself. I'm not having any physical evidence here. Speaking of which…"

He gestured with the brown envelope, and I took the envelope and opened it, part of my concentration focused on my Mask. Within the envelope was a small black thumb drive, and a slip of paper with a long string of letters and numbers.

"That's the encryption key to access the drive," said Niles. "Don't lose that paper. It's the only copy of the key. I didn't even keep one."

"No physical evidence," I said, returning the drive and the paper to the envelope. "And no files left on your servers."

"Precisely," said Niles. "Though of course I do not operate any unlicensed server-class computer systems, and have never once considered breaking the law for any reason whatsoever."

"Nor have I," I said, lying just as much as he was.

Niles waved a thick hand at me. "But everything you need is on the drive. The blueprints, and the template file for the invitation. Just make sure you find a printer that can do the holographic code on the bottom."

"Thank you," I said. "Always a pleasure during business with you."

I turned to go.

"One other thing," said Niles.

I turned again, fighting down a stab of irritation. Turning while Masked was always extra work.

"What, do you want more money?" I said.

"I wouldn't object," said Niles, "but you need to know something. There's a blank spot on the plans."

I made my Masked face scowl. "You charged me for incomplete blueprints?"

"Of course not," said Niles. He leaned forward, his chair giving an alarming creak. "Those are the complete blueprints. There's just a large blank space in the center of the mansion, which means…"

"Which means McCade built part of his house off the books," I said. I was certain that when I looked at the plans, the blank spot would correspond with the vault door in his library.

"Yeah," said Niles. "If you're getting involved with a guy like Paul McCade, you should be careful. He has a bad reputation."

"Did you get food poisoning from a McCade canned meat product?" I said.

"The stuff tastes better than it sounds," said Niles. "But that's not the point. In certain illegal circles, shall we say, McCade has a bad reputation. He likes to buy up stolen artwork and relics, and I've heard a rumor that he even does business with Rebel cells."

"That seems unlikely," I said, though not even Morvilind had been certain if McCade dealt with Rebels. "The Inquisition doesn't screw around with Rebels. If a rich guy like McCade started doing business with a Rebel cell, the Inquisition would kill him and stick the video up on Punishment Day. "

"The Inquisition is fearsome, but not omniscient," said Niles. "That's how men like you and I are in business. And a man like McCade has many friends in Homeland Security and the Elven nobility, which means he has space to do things quietly." He shrugged. "Do as you wish. But you're a reliable customer, and I would hate to lose the income stream."

I laughed. "You're getting sentimental."

"A weakness of mine," he said. "Do take care. But bear in mind that if you get arrested, I've never met you."

"Same goes," I said, waved goodbye, and walked out of his office. The receptionist did not look as I passed, and I left the office and headed into the street. Part of my attention maintained the Mask, but the rest of my mind chewed over what Niles had told me. Was McCade a Rebel? Or was he working with them? I didn't care about the Rebels and their mad plans to overthrow the High Queen, but I needed to get that stupid tablet for Morvilind and get out alive. It would be a lot harder to do that if I walked into some murky political intrigue. I muttered curses under my breath as I walked, venting my anger at Morvilind, at McCade, at the Elves, and the whole damned world.

A few blocks later I turned into an alley between office buildings, making my way through a maze of parking lots and side streets. I planned to walk to one of the bus stops near the freeway and take the bus home. Then I would examine the data on the thumb drive and consider my next course of action. I had mapped out a plan for getting into McCade's vault during the gala, but I needed more details.

I stopped and looked around. I was in an alley, and there was no one nearby. It should be safe to let my Mask dissipate. I released the spell and the illusion vanished, drifting away like smoke. Relief went through me, and I sighed and took a few deep breaths. Maintaining a Mask wasn't hard, but it was a constant effort. Sort of like carrying a cinder block around with you. Which, come to think of it, sounded like a good workout idea…

I shook my head, crossed another parking lot, ducked into an alley, and froze.

The man with the sweatshirt and the wrap-around sunglasses was walking down the center of the alley, no more than twenty yards away. It was the same man I had seen outside of McCade's mansion, I was sure of it. Up close, he looked lean and tough, moving with the confident stride of a man who knew how to handle himself.

He took one more step, saw me, and froze. The big sunglasses concealed much of his expression, but I could tell that he recognized me and that he hadn't expected to see me here.

For a moment we stared at each other, my heart pounding, my head racing with a dozen different plans.

He spoke first.

"What's a pretty girl like you doing in an alley like this?" he said. His voice was flat, unemotional.

"Seriously?" I said. "You're going with that? Bit clichéd, isn't it? Next you'll tell me it was a dark and stormy night."

"I saw you at McCade's mansion," said the man. "You were on the cleaning crew."

"Or are you hitting on me?" I said. "Are you going to tell me that heaven must be missing an angel? That'll work. Women love getting hit on by weird guys with sunglasses in alleys."

I had the pleasure of seeing his mouth tighten with annoyance. "No, you were there, with the cleaning crew."

"Don't know what you're talking about," I said. "I've never cleaned a day in my life. I don't even do laundry. I just buy new clothes when the old ones get dirty."

"You were at the mansion," said the man, "and then you followed me here."

I blinked. He thought that I had followed him?

"Don't be ridiculous," I said. "I didn't follow you. I just want to be left alone."

"You've been following me," he said. "Why?"

I couldn't see any weapons on him, but he could have a knife or a small gun tucked away in that baggy sweatshirt. For that matter, he looked like he was in good shape. I was in good shape, too, but he stood a foot taller than me and outweighed me by fifty or sixty pounds. If he had any fighting experience at all, he wouldn't need a gun or a knife to handle me.

"I haven't been following you," I said, "and I've never seen you before in my life. I'd remember those stupid sunglasses."

His mouth twitched a little. "They help my eyes."

"Well, goody for you," I said. "Why don't you go help your eyes somewhere else?"

"You're going to answer some questions for me," said the man.

"Okay," I said. "Fine. What do you want to know? I…"

I flinched and took a step back, my eyes going wide.

It was an old, old trick, but sometimes the old tricks work. The man half-turned, and as he did, I whirled and sprinted as fast as I could, grateful that I had not chosen a disguise that required high heels. I had reached the end of the alley before he got himself collected and started pursuit.

He was fast. Like, professional athlete fast. I had a good lead, but he was going to catch me. I couldn't fight him off.

Which meant I was going to have to get clever.

I tore around the corner into an alley between a strip mall and an office building. Dumpsters stood here and there, and closed steel doors led into the back rooms of the various mall shops. I had maybe six seconds before my pursuer came around the corner. I stopped, put my back to the wall, and took a deep breath, trying to clear my mind and summon magical power.

Then I cast the Cloak spell.

Cloaking was hard, really hard. When Masking, I could move around and interact with people. Cloaking took the entirety of my concentration and willpower. It was a bit like doing a deadlift at the limits of your strength – it took everything I had to do it.

But I did it.

Silver light flashed around me, and the world went hazy and indistinct, like a sheet of cloudy glass had fallen over my vision. While the Cloak spell was in place, I was completely invisible. No one could see me, and no magical spell could detect my presence.

I just couldn't do anything else while I maintained the Cloak.

My pursuer came around the corner maybe a second and a half later. He ran past me, then stopped, his face turning back and forth as he tried to find me. I took deep, controlled breaths, focused on holding the Cloak. Working the Cloak had been difficult. Maintaining the Cloak got harder with every passing second. It was a lot like holding a barbell over my head – hard at first, and getting more difficult.

The man took three quick steps back, his sunglasses swiveling back and forth, and came to a stop two feet away from me. I could have reached out and touched him. Up close, he looked handsome in a lean sort of way beneath the big sunglasses, and for an absurd instant I wondered what color his eyes were. He had a ragged shock of brown hair above the sunglasses, his brow furrowed as he looked back and forth.

I noticed something else, too. He didn't have a shadow. At this time of day, the dumpsters cast shadows. I had a shadow, too, though the Cloak hid it. Yet he didn't have one. That was bad. I had heard rumors of men without shadows, and none of them were good.

For now, though, the man with no shadow looked puzzled. To his perspective, I had just disappeared. There hadn't been enough time to force open one of the doors or to climb up the wall to the roof. His gaze turned towards the nearest dumpster, his frown tightening. Likely he thought that I had hidden myself among the trash bags. I expected him to stride forward and search the dumpster, and then depart the alley. That would take no more than a few moments, and I could maintain my Cloak that long.

Instead he lifted his right hand, gesturing with his left, and tiny arcs of lightning snarled around the fingers of his right hand, harsh and blue-white.

The man was a wizard.

He pushed out his right hand, and the arcs of lightning burst from his fingers and jumped to strike the dumpster, wrapping around it with a crackling hiss. The man strode forward as the lightning faded away, reached up, and flipped the lid open to rummage through the trash bags.

I started to shake from the effort of maintaining the Cloak.

At last the man with no shadow stepped back and looked around once more, his frustration plain.

"How in the hell did she do that?" he muttered.

That gave me a little jolt of satisfaction. I tried to use it to maintain the Cloak. The man cast another spell, one I recognized. It was the spell to detect the presence of magic. It would have worked to detect a Mask (one of the reasons I couldn't use it with Elves or other wizards), but the Cloak shielded me from detection spells. The man swept his hand back and forth and found nothing. He gave another annoyed shake of his head, turned, and stalked from the alley.

I was alone again.

I made myself count to three hundred, my shoulders and legs shuddering with the effort of maintaining the Cloak. The man did not return, and at last I let the Cloak dissipate, the magic fading away. I wanted to sit down and take a nap, but I made myself turn and walk, gathering energy for another spell. I whispered in Elven and worked another Mask, making myself look like an elderly woman in a tracksuit and sneakers. If the man with the sunglasses saw me from a distance, he would only see an old woman out for a walk. The effort made my head throb with pain, but I dared not lower the Mask.

I did not release the Mask until I got on the bus, got off at the stop near my apartment, and made sure that no one was nearby. A wave of dizziness went over me, and I just barely managed to get into my apartment before I slumped against the wall and slid to the floor, breathing hard.

A wave of despair went through me. Morvilind would work spells like this with barely an effort, and I felt as exhausted as if I had run a marathon. How could I ever break free of him if I could not even do this?

I pushed aside the despair. One problem at a time. First, I had to steal the tablet from McCade. I had to avoid McCade's security and the strange man in the sunglasses, whoever or whatever he was. Then I could worry about other things.

Yes. One problem at a time. Easiest thing in the world, right?

It was a long time before I could stand up again.

CHAPTER 4
DANCE

The time to the Conquest Day gala flew by.

Conquest Day is on July 4th, at least in the United States. It's different in other countries. In Russia, it's on the anniversary of Red October. In the United Kingdom, Conquest Day falls on the anniversary of the Battle of Hastings. It's on July 4th in the United States because that was the day three hundred odd years ago that the High Queen executed the President and Congress on live television.

I spent the time preparing.

I kept up my façade at both Duncan Catering and EZClean Cleaners, helping to make appetizers and cakes in the morning and cleaning houses at night. The next time the EZClean crew went to McCade's mansion for its weekly cleaning, I volunteered to do the art gallery and the library. Since both tasks were so unpleasant, the shift supervisor accepted without complaint. That meant I was alone in the library for a few moments. The security men had checked us over thoroughly, complete with metal detectors. A vacuum cleaner set off the metal detectors, but that was to be expected.

Which meant that the small duffel bag I concealed in the vacuum's cylinder was not detected. Halfway through vacuuming the library, I used my levitation spell to float to the top of the high shelves on the first floor of the library, in the corner where none of the cameras reached, and duct-taped the bag on the top of the shelf, out of sight from the floor and the second-story balcony.

The week after that, I used my levitation spell to float up and check the duffel bag again. The bag had not been disturbed, and I was confident that it would be there on the night of the gala.

Better and better.

At Duncan Catering Company, I got myself assigned to the crew scheduled to serve the food at McCade's gala. We would take one of the company's big white vans to the mansion, and I had noticed that while the security men always screened the workers, they never bothered to check any vehicles in the utility garage. That was a mistake, because it meant the duffel bag I taped to the bottom of the van would not be noticed.

When I wasn't working at one of my two full-time jobs, I prepared in other ways. A printer that could print an intricate holographic design like McCade's party invitation cost upward of fifteen thousand dollars. I wasn't about to spend that much money, and computer equipment like that had to be licensed with Homeland Security. So I found a print shop, broke in one night, and borrowed their printer to print the invitation. Once I finished, I used a magnet to wreck the computer's hard drive. The unfortunate owners would assume that the computer had crashed, which in turn had messed up the printer's page count.

Hopefully they had good backups.

Once that was done, I spent the rest of my time going over the plans to McCade's mansion, committing them to memory, and practicing the spells I needed. I also made contingency plans in case the job went sour and I had to run for my life. I had a storage unit out in the edge of Wauwatosa, not far from the freeway, and I stocked it with canned food and other supplies if I needed a place to hide. Of course, if the job went really bad, and if I was taken prisoner, Morvilind would use that vial of blood to kill me and dispose of any evidence of his involvement. Or McCade's security people would just shoot me on the spot. The money I had left behind for Russell might help James and Lucy…but if they could not find another Elven noble willing to treat his frostfever…

Well. That settled it. I just had to get in and out of the mansion alive. Easy as pie, right?

The biggest unknown variable was whatever waited behind that vault door in the library. The plans for the vault were not in the mansion's blueprints. Bypassing the door would be easy enough – Morvilind had taught me a great deal about the magic of releasing locks – but I had no idea what waited behind the vault door.

The second unknown variable was the strange man with no shadow. I had my suspicions, but I didn't know who or what he was. He seemed to think that I had been following him. That was absurd – I had enough trouble without asking for more. Yet that made me wonder if he had business of his own in McCade's mansion.

Maybe someone else had hired him to steal the tablet.

That could be dicey.

I would just have to keep my wits about me.

###

At last Conquest Day came.

It rained all morning and most of the afternoon, the sort of heavy, hard summer rain that made everything smell like a gym locker. It slowed to a drizzle by the time I parked my old Duluth Car Company sedan a few blocks from the Duncan Catering building. I walked to the building, sweating a little in the humidity. If anyone asked, I would claim that I had taken the bus to work. I wanted to keep the sedan nearby in case I had to make a quick escape. I had already made arrangements for an escape vehicle near McCade's mansion, but a backup never hurt.

The other servers and I changed into our formal uniforms, white shirts, slender black ties, black slacks, and shiny black shoes. At least they were flats, thank God. I pretended to tie my shoe just long enough to make sure my little duffle bag was still taped to the bottom of the van, and then I joined the others. Once we were ready, we loaded the food into the van, climbed in, and drove across Milwaukee to McCade's mansion.

We got to McCade's mansion at half past six, parking the van in its usual spot in the utility garage. The security men stood guard at the doors, and subjected us to the customary weapons scan and search. I made sure not to bring a phone, so they didn't confiscate it. The less evidence I left behind, the better. It took a dozen trips to bring everything up to the mansion's kitchen, a vast expanse of gleaming white tile and polished steel about six times the size of my apartment. It took us the better part of an hour to get everything set up, and another twenty minutes to get the food properly heated.

Then it was almost eight o'clock, which meant it was time to serve hors d'oeuvres to McCade's guests.

I put on my friendliest smile, picked up a tray loaded with shrimp puffs, and walked with the others to meet the wealthiest and the most powerful of the Midwest.

Already a substantial crowd had gathered in the glassed-in courtyard. Pale silver and blue mood lighting played over everything, and a hidden projector threw a scene onto the glass, an image of the High Queen's banner rippling in the breeze, an American flag flying below it. I had to admit it made for an impressive sight. Already men in expensive black suits and women in sleek black dresses and high heels stood talking. Here and there I saw a man in the blue officer's uniform of Homeland Security, and a few in the black-trimmed red uniform of the Wizards' Legion. I recognized several men as ambassadors from the various client states of the European Union and others from the Chinese Imperium. I suppose McCade's meat products had fans overseas. There were even a few minor Elven nobles already, mostly knights and barons from the United States and the European Union, standing aloof and cold from the human guests, their gaunt, pale faces masks of hauteur. The Elven men wore long blue coats that hung to their knees, their ornamented red cloaks thrown back, while the women wore shimmering gowns of green and blue. Two of the Elven nobles were Knights of the Inquisition, stark in their long black coats with silver lightning bolts upon their collars, and even the other Elves avoided the Inquisitors.

Had I used a Mask, every wizard and every Elf in the courtyard would have sensed it at once. Just as well I had employed a more mundane disguise.

Besides, when you're pretending to be a waiter, it's like you're invisible.

So long as you don't spill anything, of course.

I circulated through my assigned segment of the courtyard, the silver tray with the shrimp puffs balanced upon my left hand. The damned thing was heavier than it looked, and I was grateful for all the hours I had spent doing push-ups, pull-ups, and deadlifts. Granted, I hadn't thought I would put my strength training to use carrying a tray of shrimp, but I wasn't going to complain. I made sure to start with the Elves (I definitely did need an accusation of elfophobia just now), bowing as I offered them the tray. Only one of the Elven nobles deigned to take a shrimp puff, and then I moved through the human dignitaries. The shrimp proved more popular there, and soon my tray was empty. One man in particular, a stout Homeland Security major whose blue uniform made his paunch look distressingly like a blueberry, took five puffs. He then continued his inebriated flirtation with an annoyed-looking blond woman at least fifteen years his junior.

I made sure to remember him for later.

Once the last shrimp puff had been claimed, I circled the edge of the courtyard and vanished into the kitchens. Orderly chaos reigned in the kitchens, with thirty different men and women hurrying about their tasks, some of them cooking more food, other refilling trays, others pouring champagne into glasses. I slipped past them, tucked my tray under my arm, and headed down the stairs to the utility garage. Only one security guard remained on watch, a bored expression on his face as he played a game on his phone, and he glanced up at me.

"Someone spilled bleach on the tray," I said. "Have to get a new one."

The guard grunted and looked back at his phone.

I passed him, returned to the van, and put the tray in its place. I glanced around, made sure I was out of the cameras' fields of view, and yanked my duffle bag from beneath the car. I opened it up, checked its contents one more time.

Then I stripped down to my underwear, tossing my clothes into the van's laundry bin. My next outfit came out of the duffel bag – a sleeveless black dress with a short, tight skirt, and a pair of black shoes with four-inch heels. I quickly slapped earrings in place and dropped a silver necklace over my head, and then undid my ponytail, letting my hair fall loose around my shoulders. Makeup would have been ideal, but there wasn't time to apply it, and the light was dim in the courtyard anyway. I did apply some perfume to hide the smells of the kitchen. I flipped the duffel bag inside out, revealing its shiny interior and transforming it into a hideously ugly purse, and reloaded the remaining contents. I stepped to the driver's side mirror and gave myself a quick look. I looked like someone's spoiled daughter, which was perfect.

I cast the Masking spell, making myself appear as a male catering worker in white shirt and black pants, and hastened across the parking garage. I had to take care to Mask the loud clicks of my heels with every stride. Fortunately, it was a wasted effort. The guard did not look up from his phone, and security cameras could not penetrate a Mask. Anyone watching through the cameras in the garage or reviewing the footage later would see nothing amiss.

I left the garage, dropped my Mask, and crossed the mansion's lush lawn, acres of brilliant green grass trimmed with machine-like precision, and made for the glassed-in courtyard. A crowd of later arrivals filed through the doors to the courtyard, and four of McCade's security men stood there. I joined the crowd, adjusting the straps of my fake purse, and walked towards the door.

"Miss?" One of the guards, a middle-aged man with the look of a veteran still familiar with violence, held out his hand.

"What?" I said, filling my tone with surly truculence.

"This is a private party, miss," said the guard. "I need to see your invitation."

"Oh my God!" I said, letting my voice go up an octave. "Don't you know who I am?" A few of the other guests looked at me and snickered.

"Unfortunately I do not, miss," said the guard, "which is why I need to see your invitation."

"My daddy is so going to get you fired," I said. "He's friends with the Duke of Milwaukee, and you're just a security guard. You can't talk to me that way."

"Please present your invitation, miss," said the guard, still polite. My disguise was working. Had he thought me a random party crasher, he would have used force by now.

"Just do as he says, dear," said a middle-aged woman in an elegant black gown.

"Fine," I said, drawing the word into an angry whine. I reached into my purse, drew out the fake invitation, and unfolded it. "Will you let me inside? I haven't eaten all day."

The guard lifted his phone. The usual camera had been augmented with some kind of fancy combined IR/UV lens. He waved the phone over the bottom of the invitation, and I briefly saw the holographic seal and its embedded barcode flash. I hoped that Niles had done his work right, and that the printer I had "borrowed" had been up to the task.

The phone beeped, and the guard glanced at the display.

"Please enjoy the party, Miss Annovich," he said.

I sniffed and walked past him, letting my heels click loudly, and the guard forgot about me as he turned to the other guests.

More people had arrived while I had been changing clothes, and now close to a thousand guests occupied the courtyard. The air conditioning was on full blast, the air chilly against my bare arms and calves. Across the courtyard, I saw a good-sized crowd spilling into the art gallery, admiring McCade's collection. I wanted to slip away from the gala and reach the library, and do it without drawing undue notice. I reached into my purse and felt the smooth plastic of the burner phone I had prepared. I just needed to find that drunken Homeland Security major, and I would…

Speakers crackled overhead, and suddenly a voice boomed in my ears.

"Ladies, gentlemen, honored guests, and nobles of the High Queen's court," said a man's voice. "If I might have your attention for a moment?"

The lights swiveled overhead, falling upon a clear spot near the art gallery. For the first time, I looked upon Paul McCade in the flesh. Morvilind's photographs had given me a good impression of the man. He wore an extremely expensive suit, the coat cut a little longer in imitation of Elven fashion, though it didn't quite conceal his small paunch. His graying hair was perfectly parted on the left, and he wore rimless glasses perched upon his nose. He was handsome in a sort of dry, passionless way, and the owner of McCade Foods looked like a man who had never touched a McCade Foods product in his life.

I didn't like him. Just as well. It's always harder to steal from people you like.

"It is with great pleasure that I welcome you to my home on this Conquest Day, the three hundred and fourteenth anniversary since our wise and gracious High Queen brought the benefits of her just rule and wisdom to Earth," said McCade. "In that time, look at all that mankind has accomplished under the guidance of the High Queen and her nobles. War between human nations has been outlawed. Our cities are safe and prosperous, and human men-at-arms have fought under the High Queen's banner in a hundred demesnes of the Shadowlands and upon the face of a dozen different alien worlds. We have even faced the rebel Archons and their armies of orc slaves and fouler things, and have emerged victorious. Let us look forward to the day when the High Queen at lasts defeats the Archons and returns to her home, and the Elven and human races alike shall prosper under her wise hand. To the Day of Restoration!"

"The Day of Restoration!" we responded, automatically, followed by the Pledge of Allegiance to the United States and the High Queen (the foreign guests did not participate, but bowed their heads respectfully). It was one of the things you learned in school. At least, normal people did, though Morvilind's tutors had taught me how to mimic normal people reasonably well.

"My friends," said McCade once we had finished, "McCade Foods has the great honor of providing our fighting men with rations. In their honor, and for the honor of our glorious High Queen, I invite you to celebrate Conquest Day!"

The crowd applauded, and McCade waved for a moment, then hurried over to speak with the Elven nobles. I saw that Tamirlas, the Duke of Milwaukee himself, had arrived, a tall Elven noble in a gold-trimmed blue coat, his profile stark and forbidding. The hidden speakers began to play music, and some people broke into pairs to dance, while others went to bother my former coworkers at the catering company for more food. I turned, seeking for the Homeland Security major I had spotted earlier…

A tall man in a tuxedo stepped into my line of sight. Likely he wanted to dance. I flashed him a polite smile and started to step past him.

"Care to dance?"

The voice froze me in place, and I turned, keeping my smile in place.

It was the man without a shadow who had pursued me near Niles's office.

I took a long look at him.

He…cleaned up pretty nicely, actually.

Without the sunglasses, I got a good look at his face. It was lean with sharp cheekbones, and deep brown eyes the color of expensive bookcases. His brown hair had been styled and trimmed, glinting in the light from overhead. His tuxedo was, perhaps, a bit too snug, but he had the physique to make it look good. I couldn't see any weapons on him, but he could have a folding knife or a small gun tucked away in the pockets of his coat.

Of course, he could use magic, could call the lightning to his grasp. With that kind of power, he didn't really need to bother with a gun.

He met my gaze without flinching, and I felt a strange sort of pressure from his eyes.

"Why?" I said.

He shrugged. "A man sees a pretty girl at a gala, he asks her to dance. I imagine it is the sort of thing one does." His thin lips moved into a smile. "It will give us a chance to talk."

I didn't think he was with McCade's security. If he was, he would have thrown me out already. It was more likely he worked for Homeland Security, or even served as a human agent for the Inquisition. Which meant that he might have been hunting for me, following up on one of the many other crimes I had committed. If that was true, I was finished.

Unless…

Unless he was a Homeland Security officer or an Inquisition agent here for McCade or one of McCade's guests. That made much more sense. The Inquisition's mission was to root out disloyalty to the High Queen, and while everyday people feared the Knights of the Inquisition, so long as people like James and Lucy paid their taxes and didn't denounce the High Queen the Inquisition let them alone. People like McCade, who had the spare money to fund a Rebel cell, had much more to fear from the Inquisition. For that matter, Elven nobles feared the Inquisitors. That was one of the reasons Morvilind kept a vial of my heart's blood. If something went wrong and I was arrested, he could kill me from a distance before the Inquisition learned of his various illegal enterprises.

And that meant the man in the tuxedo was fishing for information.

"Mmm," said the man, and I realized that I had been staring at him. "I must have something in my teeth."

"What?" I said.

"I asked you to dance, and you froze up like a deer in the headlights," said the man. He looked amused. "Though I suspect you aren't asked to dance very often."

What the hell did that mean? Then I realized he was trying to push my buttons, to get a reaction out of me. That did calm me a little. An agent for Homeland Security or the Inquisition would just arrest me on the spot. If he was playing games, that meant he wasn't sure about me…and I could play along.

"It was just unsettling," I said. "After all, you went to such lengths to chase me down. Makes a girl wonder why you want to dance with her so much."

In answer, he held out his hand. I took it, putting my other hand on his shoulder, while his free hand settled upon my hip. His fingers felt a little cold, but that might have been the air conditioning. The music playing from the courtyard's speakers was pleasant but bland, and we moved in a slow circle as we danced.

I watched him, waiting for him to speak first.

"What's your name?" he said at last.

"Katerina Annovich," I said.

"Is it really?" he said.

I raised an eyebrow. "That's what it says on the invitation."

"Your completely accurate invitation, I'm sure," said the man.

"So what's your name?" I said. "Tall, dark, and laconic? Hard to fit on a driver's license."

"My name is Corvus."

I laughed at that. "Is it really? Corvus? Latin word for crow? Very dramatic. Do you dress all in black and listen to sad music?"

To his credit, he did not even bat an eye. "Only on weekends."

"Well, Mr. Corvus," I said, "why don't you tell me something? How did you do that trick with the shadow?"

"I don't know what you mean," Corvus said, his expression cooling a little.

"You don't have a shadow," I said. "Hard to tell in here, and I doubt anyone will notice." The shoulder under my hand tensed, though his expression remained amused. "So, what's your story? Are you a vampire? I read in some old book that vampires don't have shadows."

"No such thing as vampires," said Corvus.

"Nope," I said. "Worse things, though. Some of them don't have shadows."

"Why don't we make a deal?" said Corvus. "I'll tell you why I don't have a shadow, but you'll tell me how you got out of that alley."

I gave him a sunny smile. "I don't know what you mean."

"I bet if I talked to Paul McCade and asked to see his guest list," said Corvus, "that I wouldn't find anyone named Katerina Annovich in the file."

I kept the sunny smile in place. "What about a man named Corvus?"

"An agent of the Inquisition," said Corvus, "would find it a simple matter to edit the guest list, would she not?"

"So he would," I said. "I…wait." I blinked as my brain caught up to what he had said. "She would find it simple? Wait. You think I'm an agent of the Inquisition?"

"The thought had crossed my mind," said Corvus.

"My God," I said. "That suit's so tight that the circulation to your brain has stopped. You really think I'm an agent of the Inquisition? Or that I'm with Homeland Security?"

"Homeland Security is too stupid to deal with someone like me," said Corvus. "You seriously thought I was an Inquisitor?"

I shrugged, which was harder to do while dancing than I thought. "Why else would you chase me down?"

"Really, you should have more confidence in your appearance," said Corvus. "You must have men chasing you all the time."

"Not for the reasons you might think," I said.

"I'll let you in on a little secret," said Corvus.

He tugged on my arms, and suddenly I was pressed against him. He was a lot stronger than he looked. I was suddenly very aware of his hands against me for two reasons. First, he could kill me, and I wouldn't be able to stop him. Second, he could…do pretty much anything else he wanted.

I shoved that thought right out of my mind.

He leaned closer, his breath against my right ear.

"Every Inquisitor," said Corvus, "still has his shadow."

He stepped back and spun me, and I was just able to keep my balance by flinging out my right arm. I supposed it looked graceful, and we drew a few appreciative claps from the nearby guests.

For a moment we stared at each other, still gripping hands

"Why don't we agree," I said, "to say out of each other's way? Whatever your reasons for coming here…I'm sure they're not mine."

"I think we can agree on that," said Corvus. "Good fortune to you, Miss Annovich."

"And to you, Mr. Corvus."

He smiled once more, planted a cold, dry kiss onto my fingers, and strolled off into the crowd. I watched him go.

The tuxedo did fit him well. It annoyed me that I noticed it. That kind of physical attraction was a liability, could cause me to make stupid mistakes. Morvilind had too much power over me already, and a romantic relationship with a man would cause me to give up even more power over my fate.

I had learned that one the hard way.

Well, it didn't matter. I didn't know if he was an Inquisitor or a Homeland Security officer or something else, but clearly I was not his objective. It occurred to me that Corvus had been near Niles Ringer's office to buy a forged invitation for himself, and we had just stumbled into each other by bad luck.

It also occurred to me that he might be here to do something illegal himself, maybe to steal something.

Or to kill someone.

His lack of a shadow…

I pushed that thought aside. It wasn't my problem, and I had my own concerns to manage. Specifically, I needed to get my hands on that tablet and get out of here before anyone noticed it was gone.

I headed across the courtyard, my eyes darting back and forth, and I found the middle-aged Homeland Security major I had spotted earlier. He was drinking another glass of champagne, and to judge from the ruddy color of his face, he had downed another two or three glasses while I had been chatting with Corvus.

Perfect.

I reached into my fake purse, tapped a few commands into a burner phone, and then glided over to talk to him, my eyes wide, my back ramrod straight and my shoulders back to emphasize my chest as I asked him to dance. That did the trick. I caught his eye at once, and soon had his undivided attention. I learned that his name was Major Colin Kemp, that he had multiple awards for arresting Rebel terrorists, and that neither his wife nor his ungrateful children nor his commanding officer appreciated all his hard work. I nodded in agreement, touching his arm as I laughed at his jokes. Someone like Corvus would have seen through me at once. Maybe Major Kemp was a bit savvier when he was sober, but soon he was doing exactly what I wanted.

A kiss on his cheek persuaded him, and soon we were walking arm and arm across the courtyard and into the art gallery. The gallery was much less crowded than the courtyard proper, likely because a pair of polite but unsmiling security men kept anyone from bringing food and drink. Likely McCade did not want his masterpieces damaged with shrimp sauce and champagne. Here and there men and women stood in small clumps, admiring the sculptures.

"Let's go someplace quiet," said Major Kemp. "Maybe that library?" He jerked his head toward the double wooden doors to the library, one of which stood slightly ajar. "We can…talk."

"That sounds nice," I said. "You have such interesting stories. I think…"

Right on time, my burner phone went off. I made a show of rolling my eyes and reaching into my purse. Of course, the phone wasn't really ringing. I had installed Niles Ringer's fake call app, and to my surprise it had turned out to be clever. It even simulated a fake voice over the phone's speaker, so anyone listening in wouldn't realize the fraud.

"Daddy?" I said into the phone, and Major Kemp's eyes widened. "Oh. My. God! You are such a jerk! Like, I don't even have school until Monday. So what if I don't graduate high school?"

"High school?" said Major Kemp, his eyes going even wider.

I waved a dismissive hand and smiled at him, and starting shrieking into my phone again. "Don't tell me that! I don't care what you think! I'm going to do what I want…"

Self-preservation conquered Major's Kemp libido. He turned and walked away as fast as he could while still maintaining something that resembled dignity. No one took any notice of me as Kemp hurried away.

I closed the fake call app, dropped the phone back into my purse, and made my way into McCade's library.

CHAPTER 5
THE PRIVATE PARTY

My heels made no noise against the library's thick carpet.

I paused just beyond the door and looked around, my eyes sweeping over the balconies and the shelves. The library was deserted for the moment, and I saw no one in the main floor, the balconies, or in one of the side rooms that housed the various rare books. That would not last, though. Major Kemp had thought the library a perfect place for a dalliance, and other lechers might have the same thought. I glanced at the ceiling and the railing, noting the location of the cameras. Their position and alignment had not changed since the last time I had vacuumed the library.

Which meant I knew where I could walk to avoid their field of vision.

I skirted the edge of the lower floor, keeping close to the wooden shelves of books. I reached the corner, looked around, and summoned magical power, working it into a spell. The levitation spell took hold of me, and I floated towards the top of the shelf. I had a stab of irrational fear that someone might try to look up my skirt, but there was no one around.

And I had far more serious things to worry about.

The duffel bag remained in place. I pulled it loose, and as I did, I noticed something odd.

The nearest camera had been disconnected.

I blinked and took a harder look at the thing. The camera was mounted in a little dome of black plastic, but I saw where the network cable had been unplugged. It wasn't a wireless camera – the model was wrong for that. Maybe that camera had been damaged, but a quick glance around proved otherwise.

All the cameras in the library had been unplugged.

It made absolutely no sense at all. If those cameras were unplugged, the security men ought to have been swarming over the library. Except those cameras were forty feet off the floor. You needed a ladder and a good screwdriver, or a good screwdriver and a levitation spell, to unplug all those cameras.

Which meant…

Which meant that Paul McCade knew that the cameras had been unplugged. Which in turn meant he had ordered them unplugged.

Why?

Had he known I was coming? If he had known I was planning to rob him, the security men would have shot me on sight, or he would have had Homeland Security arrest me, and I would wait to see if Morvilind would kill me before I wound up naked and flogged on a Punishment Day video. Odds were that Paul McCade did not even know I existed.

Something else was going on. Something that, in all probability, did not involve me at all. My problems were not the center of the universe.

Outrageous as that might be.

I floated back to the floor and released the levitation spell. Another look around the library, and then I slipped into one of the side rooms, the one holding the collection of Mark Twain first editions. I opened the duffel bag I had taken from the shelf and pulled out a pair of black cargo pants, black socks, and black running shoes. I slipped off my heels and donned the new clothes. Wearing cargo pants with a black cocktail dress looked peculiar, but I had used the combination before. I stuffed various useful items into the pockets and put my high heels and my fake purse into the duffel bag, adjusting the straps to turn it into an impromptu backpack. Best not to leave any physical evidence behind.

I strode back into the main floor of the library, towards the vault door, and I froze in surprise.

The vault door was unlocked.

It had likely been unlocked the entire time I had been in the library. First the cameras, and now the vault door? Just what was going on?

Voices came from the library door.

I was caught between two easy chairs, and I had no time to hide, no time to run. I summoned power and cast a Cloak around myself. An instant later two men in the blue uniforms of Homeland Security officers entered the library. I tensed, fearing they had come for me, but neither man had drawn his sidearm, and both looked at least a little drunk. The officers walked to the vault door and pulled, and it swung open a few feet, pale blue light spilling into the library. I caught a brief whiff of something that smelled like…smoke? Incense?

Then the officers vanished into the blue light.

No one else came into the library, so I dropped my Cloak with a shudder of relief. For a moment I hesitated, trying to decide upon a course of action. Perhaps it was time to scrap this plan and start over. Things were happening here that I did not understand. I saw again the large blank spot in the mansion's plan. McCade had secrets here, and if I wasn't careful, those secrets were going to get me killed.

Of course, if I didn't retrieve the tablet for Morvilind, I might get killed anyway. If I failed, he might simply tell me to try again. Or he might have me killed to cover his tracks. And McCade had unplugged his own security cameras. That meant there was something happening that he didn't want recorded, that he wanted kept secret. I could exploit his need for secrecy, and make off with the tablet before anyone could stop me. This might be my best opportunity for success.

I nodded to myself, took a deep breath, and summoned power, reading myself to Cloak or Mask if necessary. An Elf or a human wizard would sense a Mask, but if I was quick, I could Cloak before anyone noticed me. And if there were no wizards in the vault, then I could Mask myself as a Homeland Security officer and stroll right through them.

I crossed the library to the massive vault door, slipping past the enormous slab of steel to find myself in…

Not a vault.

For a moment I looked around, bewildered.

From time to time the Department of Education put out videos describing what Earth had been like in the final few decades before the Conquest, describing the moral decay and corruption of Earth's governments before the High Queen had arrived to guide mankind. Usually those videos portrayed pre-Conquest Earth as a hellhole of poverty and despair and squalor where the poor starved and died in meaningless wars while the rich led lives of debauchery and wanton immorality. The videos invariably included a few seconds of actors in expensive suits and actresses in skimpy dresses, dancing and drinking in a dim room while bad music played in the background.

I didn't know or care whether or not that was a true view of pre-Conquest Earth, but the room beyond the vault door looked almost exactly like one of those videos.

Dim blue light bathed everything, reflecting off the polished white floor and gleaming steel tables. A dull bass beat pulsed from hidden speakers. There were close to a hundred men and women in the room, some of them dancing, some of them drinking or smoking from pipes. The smell of the smoke had a sharp edge to it, and I suspected they were not smoking tobacco. Couches rested here and there, and the guests lay upon them, some of them glassy-eyed, others giggling and whispering to themselves as various drugs took hold.

Ah. This was Paul McCade's private party. The party for his friends, the one he didn't show to the rest of the rabble in the courtyard. No wondered he had unplugged his cameras.

"Mistress?"

A pale woman about my own age tottered over to me. She wore a ridiculously high pair of heels, a red silk kimono that barely reached the top of her thighs, and as far as I could tell, nothing else. A string of Elven hieroglyphics had been tattooed upon her forehead, and I recognized the symbols of Tamirlas, the Duke of Milwaukee.

She was a slave. Under the laws of the United States, humans could not own slaves. Elves, however, could own humans slaves. According to the law, a wealthy man like McCade could not buy slaves…but sometimes Elven nobles loaned their slaves to their human favorites. McCade was friends with Tamirlas, and it seemed the Duke had lent some of his slaves to the head of McCade Foods.

I spotted maybe thirty or forty slaves among the guests. Both the men and the women wore those sleeveless red silk kimonos. It wasn't hard to guess what the guests intended to do with the slaves, either. All of the slaves were young and attractive, and even as I watched a middle-aged woman led off a glassy-eyed man in a red kimono to one of the curtained alcoves lining the room.

I thought the Rebels were idiots, but sometimes it wasn't hard to see why they were so angry.

"I have an invitation," I said to the slave, though it would look odd if I pulled it out of my impromptu backpack.

"The master's guests are welcome," said the slave, her voice slurred. I wondered how many different chemicals the poor woman had coursing through her veins. "Would you like refreshments? Champagne is available, along with many different stimulants and narcotics."

"Gosh," I said. "Aren't those, you know, illegal?"

The slave blinked. "The master is friends with his lordship the Duke, and the master has friends in Homeland Security." She looked at the two officers I had seen earlier. They reclined on one of the couches, both smoking from pipes, odd-scented smoke rising from the bowls.

"Yeah," I said. "Refreshment. Um. I'll take a glass of champagne, please." There was no way in hell I was going to drink it. God only knew what had been added to the drink. But my pants and running shoes already stood out in the strange party, and I didn't want to draw any additional attention to myself.

Though given how drunk, drugged, and stoned most of the guests looked, I could probably start singing at the top of my lungs while hopping up and down on one foot, and no one would notice.

The slave woman gave me a glass of champagne. I took it and thanked her, which seemed to surprise her. Likely she did not hear it very often. I began circulating along the edges of the room. Granted, I had to hear some of the unpleasant noises coming from the curtained alcoves, but it kept me away from the other guests on the couches. Some of them looked as if their inhibitions had been eroded by the drugs, and I didn't want to get into any fights or deal with someone like Major Kemp.

I finished my circuit of the room, noting the details. The ceiling was not high, but the room was at least twice the size of the kitchens. At the far end of the room, opposite the vault door leading to the library, was another door. It stood open, and within a saw another blue-lit hallway, leading deeper into the mansion. Specifically, it led further into the blank area on the blueprints.

Just what the hell did McCade have in here?

I wondered if McCade had built himself a private little armory or gun factory or something, and was plotting to overthrow the Duke and seize Milwaukee for himself. Though given that his favorite guests were drugging and fornicating a few yards from me, that thought seemed ridiculous. This was the behavior of a rich boy who had grown into a hedonistic middle-aged man, not a would-be Rebel terrorist.

Yet when I had been working with the cleaning crew, I had sensed several powerful items of magic behind the vault door. Clearly they had not been stored in here with the couches. Or if they had, they had been moved for the party. I needed to find them, or see if they had been moved.

I didn't see any wizards in the room, whether human or Elven, but it was always possible that a wizard of the Legion might have removed his uniform and donned a tuxedo to attend the party. Regardless, I had to take the risk. I ducked into one of the unattended alcoves and pulled the curtain shut behind me. A couch ran along the alcove's curved wall, and the air smelled faintly of smoke and liquor and sweat. I wondered if McCade ever had the cushions in cleaned, and decided not to sit down. I waited a moment, but no one followed me into the alcove.

I gestured, summoning magical power, and cast the spell to sense the presence of magical forces. Again I detected the buzzing loci of magical power I had sensed the first time I had cast the spell in the library. I gritted my teeth, trying to focus the spell. With greater degrees of skill with the detection spell, a wizard could tell the precise distance to a magical object or spell, and discern its kind and nature. I didn't have anything like that kind of skill. I only knew that there were several enchanted objects nearby, objects with powerful auras. I wished that Morvilind had bothered to tell me what the tablet's aura felt like. Then again, he knew I didn't have the skill to discern the aura, so hadn't seen any pointing in telling me. I concentrated, trying to focus the spell. I thought the auras were coming from the hallway beyond the room with the couches, and…

A sudden flare of magical power brushed against me.

It was close. No more than a few yards away. Someone was casting a spell. A detection spell, perhaps? If another wizard was casting a detection spell, he would feel my own magic…

I whispered a curse and released the spell, my heart pounding. Stupid, stupid, stupid. I should have…

The curtain to the alcove jerked open.

Corvus stood in the doorway, a dark shadow in his black tuxedo, his hand raised in the familiar gesture of the detection spell.

I remembered the lightning he had summoned in the alley. He could cast spells. Maybe our conversation in the courtyard while we danced had been a trick. Maybe he had been following me the entire time.

I waited for him to act.

CHAPTER 6
DISGUISES

Corvus did nothing, his eyes hard and unblinking as he watched me. I realized that he was waiting to see what I would do, if I would attack.

The music rumbled from the main room, and the smell of drugged smoke and the sound of laughter came through the opened curtain. So far, it seemed that Corvus was the only one who had noticed my magic.

Maybe I should take the initiative.

"You know," I said, "those were some seriously clunky sunglasses."

He blinked. "What?"

Whatever he had been expecting me to say, that obviously hadn't been it.

"Those sunglasses you wore when you were chasing me in the alley," I said. "And when you were spying on this place. I mean, don't get me wrong, I bet they were effective. But stylish they were not. My eighty-year-old grandma wears them when she drives on sunny days." Actually, I had never met any of my grandparents, but Corvus didn't need to know that. "If you wore a floral coat and a little hat with the sunglasses, it would have looked adorable."

That would have annoyed most men. Corvus didn't even blink.

"They're practical," he said. "The sun bothers my eyes."

"Because you're a vampire, right?" I said. "No shadow, doesn't like the sunlight, can use magic…"

Corvus shook his head. "There are no such things as vampires, Miss Annovich." He stepped into the alcove, letting the curtain fall closed behind him. "As long as we are discussing fashion, I could not help but notice your running shoes."

I struck a little pose, right hand on my hip. I had the distinct feeling that Corvus was a predator of some kind, and showing fear to a predator was a bad idea. "Do you? That's so nice. They go with my dress, you know."

"They also go with your pants," he said, looking at my legs, "and with the lockpick kit in your left pocket, the multitool in your hip pocket, and the spring-release lock picking gun in your lower right pocket. I am told that a lady must accessorize, but those are some peculiar accessories."

I shrugged. "More useful than these earrings."

"Indeed," said Corvus. "Though I am curious about something. You were casting a spell."

"What a flattering thing to say," I said. "A little forward, though."

"I do not refer to your charms," said Corvus. "I mean it literally. You summoned magical force from the Shadowlands, directed it with your will, shaped it into a construct, and released the bound power in a manner of your choosing."

"That's one way of putting it," I said.

"You were casting the spell to sense the presence of magical forces," said Corvus.

"So were you," I said. "If you live in a glass house, you shouldn't throw stones."

"Human women do not generally learn magic," said Corvus. "The High Queen frowns on it. The only sanctioned human wizards are the battle spell casters in the Wizards' Legion, and those are exclusively men." He watched me. "Who taught you to cast that spell?"

I sighed. "You found out my secret. I'm actually a man." I gestured at my chest. "These? Sand in a pair of bags. I do the voice by inhaling some helium, and I…"

A brief flicker of annoyance went over his face. "You have a remarkably smart mouth."

"People keep telling me that."

"It is a dangerous quality in a thief," said Corvus.

"Oh, I'm a thief now?" I said.

"Obviously," said Corvus. "You forged an invitation, concealed your tools and equipment somewhere in the mansion, and now are here to steal something from McCade or one of his cronies. It's quite clever, really. McCade's security men are reasonably competent, but they have all the intelligence of airport screeners. They couldn't handle someone like you."

"Such flattery," I said.

To my surprise, he smiled. "You had me fooled. I thought you were far more dangerous than you really were. I thought you an agent of the Inquisition or Homeland Security. Not a thief with a few tricks."

"So," I said. "What will you do now? Going to turn me in?"

Corvus shook his head. "That would be counterproductive. I thought you might interfere with my mission, but it is clear that our objectives do not overlap."

"And just what objectives are those?" I said. "You're not with the Inquisition or Homeland Security, are you?"

Something cold and dark flashed in his brown eyes. "No."

"You're not a thief, are you?" I said.

"I most certainly am not," said Corvus.

I made an impatient gesture. "Well, then, why are you here? To enjoy McCade's private party?"

He looked disgusted at the notion. "Discipline and self-control are the foundations of an ordered mind. McCade and his cronies have neither."

"They don't need discipline and self-control. They have money, drugs, and prostitutes," I said.

"The overindulgence of which inevitably leads to destruction," said Corvus.

He…had a point. I didn't want to let anyone else have power over me, and alcohol and licentiousness were an excellent way to reduce my power over myself.

"That was an inspiring little pep talk," I said. "But it doesn't explain why you are here."

"Before I continue," said Corvus, "I wish to propose a pact."

I blinked. "A pact? Like, a suicide pact? I'll have to decline."

Corvus raised an eyebrow. "If you want to kill yourself, do not let me stop you. Just let me get to a safe distance. This tuxedo is rented, and I don't want to get any blood on it."

I laughed at that.

"Before I agree to anything," I said, "why are you here? Are you here to steal stuff, too?"

"No," said Corvus. He considered for a moment. "I am working for the Duke Tamirlas of Milwaukee."

"You're one of the Duke's men-at-arms, then," I said. I suppose that explained some of the peculiar things about Corvus. Perhaps the Duke had taught him magic the way that Morvilind had taught me.

"I am not," said Corvus. "Let us say instead that I was hired by the Duke. Or, rather, my family was hired by him."

"Your family?" I said.

"Mr. McCade no longer has the Duke's complete confidence," said Corvus. "The Duke hired my family to look into the matter, and the task was given to me."

"And what task is that?" I said.

He gestured at the curtain. "This entire section of the mansion is its own little fortress. McCade only permitted his trusted guests this far, and the corridors beyond are guarded in some fashion. I am going to see if

McCade has been engaged in a…specific activity. If he has not, then I will depart without further trouble. If he has, then I will take action."

"That's very vague," I said.

"It is all that is safe to tell you," said Corvus. "I assume you are here to steal a specific item? If you were simply after money, you could have taken the valuable books from the library or stolen jewelry from the guests."

"Yes," I said. I considered what to tell him. "All right. You've given me a little of the truth, and I'll repay you in kind. McCade has a tablet, and I'm here to steal it."

Corvus blinked. "A tablet? Like a handheld computer?"

I shook my head. "No. An ancient stone tablet. It was Assyrian or something. It has a magical aura around it."

His frown sharpened. "I see. Old magic from ancient Earth? That is telling. McCade should not possess such an item."

"My employer agrees," I said, "so I was hired to steal it from him."

Though "hired" sounded much more friendly than "coerced".

"Such a valuable item will be in McCade's inner sanctum," said Corvus. "The answer to my question will lie there as well."

"Seems likely," I said.

"Our goals are complimentary, not contradictory," said Corvus. "Therefore I propose a pact. You have skills that will be useful to me, and I suspect my abilities will help you as well. We can then help each other fulfill our missions, and then go our separate ways."

I mulled that over. "Or you could be here to take the tablet for yourself, and leave me to take the blame while you escape."

"A reasonable possibility," said Corvus. "But I have no interest in money."

"Everyone has an interest in money," I said. "No one likes starving to death."

"My family provides for my needs, which are simple enough," said Corvus. "And I have no wish to acquire an artifact of dark magic."

I blinked. "Wait. What? Dark magic?"

Corvus frowned. "You didn't know?"

"Know what?" I said.

"Magic was practiced on Earth before the Conquest," said Corvus. "Thought it was exceedingly rare, and almost vanished entirely after the fall of the Roman Empire. Yet any pre-Conquest human magic was almost exclusively dark magic. Several ancient empires made use of it. The Assyrians were one of them."

"I see," I said, a cold chill going through me.

Morvilind had sent me to steal a relic of ancient dark magic?

Why would Morvilind want an ancient relic of human dark magic? I could think of several reasons, and none of them were good. I thought his interests had always been in artwork, in old relics and sculptures he could acquire without spending any money.

But if he wanted me to steal a relic of dark magic…

There were many different kinds of magic. Humans in the Wizards' Legion were allowed to learn elemental spells, fire and earth and wind and water. The Elven mages had many kinds of spells they kept to themselves, spells of illusion and mind magic and summoning creatures from the Shadowlands. Yet the High Queen forbade the Elves from wielding the darker powers – spells of necromancy and entropy, spells to call creatures from the Void beyond the Shadowlands. The Inquisition's main mission was to make sure both Elves and humans remained loyal to the High Queen, but if the Inquisition discovered any Elf wielding dark magic, they killed him.

Was that the reason Morvilind had trained me? It made a grim amount of sense. If he was interested in dark magic, if he wanted to acquire relics of dark magic, he could use me to obtain them without risking himself. If I was captured, or if I tried to surrender to the Inquisition, he could simply use the vial of heart's blood to kill me and destroy any evidence of his misdeeds.

"You really didn't know, did you," said Corvus.

"No," I said. "Let's just say my employer is not always forthcoming with information I might need. Information that might be really goddamned useful. He ought to…" I bit my tongue before the anger got carried away and I said too much.

"Yes." His thin smile held no humor. "I was once a man-at-arms. I understand the feeling."

"All right," I said, calming down. "This pact. What did you have in mind?"

He shrugged. "We help each other accomplish our missions. I care nothing for your employer or this Assyrian tablet. I simply wish to see if McCade possesses a specific item or not."

"Not the tablet," I said.

"No."

"What kind of item?" I said.

He thought for a moment. "A book."

I jerked my head toward the wall. "Library's that way."

"It is not the kind of book that he would leave lying around," said Corvus. "It would get him in a lot of trouble, even with his closest friends."

I snorted. "What, some kind of Rebel manifesto?"

"Something like that," said Corvus.

I thought about that. It seemed unlikely that a man like McCade was a Rebel, but then it also seemed unlikely that a man like McCade would build a secret orgy room behind his library. Morvilind didn't care about the

Rebels, and neither did I. If the Duke had hired Corvus and his family to expose McCade as a Rebel, then all the better for me. In the chaos, it would be easy to get away with the tablet.

"Why would you want my help?" I said at last.

Corvus raised his eyebrows. "You do not seem like a woman who is lacking in self-confidence."

"I'm not," I said. "I also think I am a woman who would be a convenient scapegoat for whatever you plan to do."

"Confident and paranoid," said Corvus. "A dangerous combination."

"When you're breaking into a mansion," I said, "there's no such thing as paranoia."

"True," said Corvus. "For you to have come this far is impressive. Your skills would be useful in achieving my mission. For that matter, my skills would be useful in accomplishing yours."

"You can call lightning," I said. "I saw that in the alley. What else can you do?"

"You don't have any weapons," said Corvus. "If you need to fight your way out, you'll need help."

"And you would do that for me?" I said.

"If you agree to help me," said Corvus.

I blew out a long breath. I suspected Corvus knew how to handle himself. If it came to a fight with McCade's security or a cell of damned Rebels, I didn't have any choice. I would have to run and Mask myself, or Cloak and hide until I could escape. In a fight, a capable ally would be welcome. Of course, it was possible this was some kind of trap, that Corvus really was an Inquisitor or a Homeland Security thug, and he was setting me up. Or he really was a thief, and planned to use me as a fall woman.

Trusting him was risky.

On the other hand, everything I had done since Morvilind had told me to steal the tablet had been a risk. And I had to succeed. If I did not retrieve that tablet, Morvilind would not continue the annual cure spells, and Russell was going to die in a lot of pain.

If working with Corvus gave me a greater chance of success, then I would work with Corvus.

"Okay," I said. "Guess we're allies. You ever break into a place like this before?"

"Once or twice," said Corvus.

"Do what I say," I said. "One wrong move and we'll bring McCade's security down on our heads. I don't care how much lightning you can call, you can't fight through all of them."

"I will follow your lead," said Corvus. I had the feeling he was patronizing me, but I decided not to push it. "What did you have in mind?"

"I stole some blueprints for this place," I said. "Behind the library is a big blank space. I thought it was just a vault, but there's more to it than that."

"Obviously," said Corvus.

"My tablet and your book, if they're illegal artifacts, are probably in the blank space," I said. "We'll have a look around, find them, and then get the hell out of here."

"A solid plan," said Corvus.

"Hope so," I said. "Let's slip away from the party and have a look around." I went to the curtain and pushed it aside an inch, peering into the blue-lit gloom of the main room. The low bass beat of the music continued, and maybe fifty more guests had filtered into the room, sprawled on the couches or dancing in the corners. I saw more guests take slaves and vanish into the alcoves, and…

I blinked and jerked back.

Three of McCade's security men moved from alcove to alcove, twitching aside the curtains and looking inside. They seemed calm and collected, but I suspected they were looking for someone or something in particular. Maybe they were looking for Corvus.

Maybe they were looking for me.

"Hell," I whispered, getting back into the alcove and letting the curtain fall back.

"What is it?" said Corvus.

"McCade's security," I said. "Checking the alcoves. Might be looking for us."

"They're probably checking to make sure no one's had a stroke or swallowed their own tongue," said Corvus. "Always embarrassing when that happens at this kind of party."

I hadn't thought of that. "Maybe. But if they're looking for us…"

I had thirty seconds before they looked in our alcove. I could Mask myself, or I could Cloak myself, but I wasn't sure I could do the same for Corvus. I did not also want to reveal the full extent of my abilities to Corvus, either. He had been surprised that I could cast the spell to detect magic. How would he react if he knew I could use illusion magic?

Best not to find out.

But how to avoid suspicion?

The idea burst into my mind.

"Kiss me," I said.

Corvus looked nonplussed. "What?"

"Kiss me," I said. "Right now."

"You cannot be serious," he said.

"What do people use these alcoves for?" I snapped. "The guards come in, see us kissing, and then move on to the next one. We…"

Corvus let out a sharp, irritated sigh. "Fine."

Before I could say anything else, before I could even react, he seized my upper arms, yanked me close, and kissed me long and hard upon the lips, and…and…

As it turned out, he was really good at it.

I had my arms around him a few heartbeats later. That was part of the disguise. It wasn't because I was really enjoying the kiss or anything like that. Or so I tried to tell myself. He hadn't been the first man I had ever kissed. There had been a fairly serious relationship when I had been eighteen that I had kept secret from both Morvilind and Russell, a relationship that had ended badly. From time to time I flirted as part of my tasks from Morvilind, and that occasionally had led to a kiss (though, thank God, I'd never had to seduce anyone). So I wasn't a stranger to this.

Corvus was just really good at it.

The curtain twitched open, and I opened one eye to see three hard-faced men in suits scowling at me. They glanced at us, looked around the alcove, and then let the curtain fall back into place as they continued their rounds. Corvus had been right. The security men were checking to make sure none of the guests had overdosed, and had thought that Corvus and I were a pair of guests who had slipped away for some casual fun.

So I could stop kissing him now.

Except…I really didn't want to.

Then I felt a presence in my mind, thoughts that murmured of hunger and need. Morvilind had taught me the rudiments of mind magic, so I knew how to recognize an intrusion in my thoughts.

Corvus was reaching into my mind.

For a long, tantalizing moment, the hunger and need seeped into me, and I wanted nothing more than to press myself against him, to rip away the coat and shirt that prevented me from touching him, to pull my dress over my head and then…

I wasn't going to let anyone have power over me ever again.

I pushed back, breathing hard, and Corvus flinched.

"Stop," I stammered. "Whatever you're doing, just…just stop."

He stared down at me, and with a shock I realized that his eyes had turned solid black, almost as if they had filled with shadows. Corvus stepped back, his breathing hard and fast, and closed his eyes. Bit by bit he slowed his breathing, the intensity fading from his expression. He braced himself against the wall with his right hand.

"What were you doing to me?" I said. "I could…feel you in my head. And your eyes…"

"Sorry," he mumbled. "When it starts…it's hard to stop."

"Said every man ever," I said.

He barked out a hoarse little laugh and opened his eyes. They had returned to their normal brown color. "I apologize. It…has been a long time since I've done that, and I got carried away in the moment."

"Um," I said, fighting off a wave of embarrassment. He might have projected something into my thoughts, but there had been something in my head eager to receive it. "It's…been a while for me, too."

Corvus closed his eyes, nodded, and opened them again.

"What happened to your eyes?" I said. "It was like they were full of shadows."

He said nothing.

"The shadows," I said. "There are shadows in your eyes, and you don't cast a shadow. Then you projected lust or whatever into my thoughts. Just…what are you?"

"I am," said Corvus, "a man on a mission. Just as you are a woman on mission. I suggest we attend to our tasks."

I nodded and got control of my emotions. "Yes. Right. Well. Shall we?"

CHAPTER 7
RIFT WAY

I held out my left arm. Corvus stared at for a moment, the sighed and threaded his arm through mine. His forearm felt strong and firm through the sleeve of his coat.

"Care to escort a lady for a stroll?" I said.

Corvus sighed. "Don't flirt."

"Yes," I agreed. "Clearly I'm much too good at it. I made your eyes turn solid black, and while I don't know what you are, I suspect it's a sign of intense arousal and…"

The sound Corvus made was somewhere between an irritated sigh and a laugh. "Has anyone ever told you that you have a smart mouth?"

"Frequently," I said. "And often."

"That's redundant," said Corvus. "Let's go."

He pushed aside the curtain, and we walked arm-in-arm into the main room. The air had taken on a noticeable chemical reek, and more guests lay sprawled on the couches, smoking and drinking as the red-clad slaves circulated with food and drink and recreational poisons. The three security men were on the far end of the room, but they did not look our way as we wove our way past the couches and the gleaming steel tables. We reached the far doorway and slipped into the hallway beyond.

The corridor did not look nearly as elaborate as the main room. The floor was polished concrete, the walls unadorned cinder blocks. Metal conduits and pipes ran along the ceiling in orange-painted racks. Every few feet a single blue light bulb burned in a metal cage, filling the corridor in long, gloomy shadows.

"Surprised you didn't draw more attention," said Corvus.

"Why's that?" I said, looking back and forth. The distant bass thrum of the music still vibrated through the concrete floor.

"You were the only one in there wearing cargo pants and running shoes," said Corvus.

"Considering some of the hallucinogenic drugs the guests have taken," I said, looking at the pipes, "cargo pants are probably the least strange thing they've seen today."

Corvus snorted. "True."

"Look," I said, pointing at the ceiling. "We won't have to worry about security cameras."

"No network conduit," Corvus said.

"Too much concrete and steel in here for wireless," I said. I reached into my pack and drew out my burner phone to check. It wasn't getting any signal, and it didn't detect any local wireless networks. "Nice and private. No cameras, no Internet, no way for anyone to call out."

"Indeed," said Corvus, his tone grim. "Quite a lot of water, though." He pointed. "Pipes for hot and cold water, and they're not part of the air conditioning system."

I scowled at the pipes. "You think he keeps prisoners back here?"

"Perhaps," said Corvus. "Though one wonders why a manufacturer of badly-flavored meat products would acquire prisoners."

"Not a fan of McCade Foods canned meat products?" I said.

Corvus frowned. "I have experienced near-starvation, so while I would prefer McCade's food products to starving again…"

"Saying food is preferable to starvation is not high praise," I said.

"No," said Corvus. "Which way should we go?"

I shrugged and pointed at the pipes. "Let's follow the hot water."

We started forward, making our way down the utility corridor. My running shoes made no sound against the floor. Corvus wore gleaming dress shoes, but somehow he walked in silence as well. That was a neat trick.

"Out of curiosity," I said, "are you a vampire?"

He rolled his eyes. "There are no such things as vampires. You've seen me in the sunlight. Some of the shrimp puffs I ate had a lot of garlic in them. I didn't bite your neck and suck out your blood while we were alone." He opened one of the buttons of his shirt and reached inside, drawing out a slender silver chain. A little golden cross hung from the end of it. "And if I remember my popular fiction correctly, vampires burn at the touch of these."

"It was resting against your undershirt," I said.

He snorted and tapped his finger against the cross, and failed to burst into flames.

"So you believe in God?" I said.

"Yes. Not all in my family do, but I do."

"Peculiar thing for people in our line of work," I said. The corridor stretched on without any doors, though I did see a corner coming up.

"You do not?" said Corvus.

"If God is supposed to be good," I said, "then why is the world full of people like Paul McCade?"

"Perhaps it is our task to improve the world," said Corvus in a quiet voice, "to cut out the evil from among its peoples as a surgeon cuts out a cancer."

"What a peculiar thing to say," I said. "Do you know a spell that can sense anyone nearby?"

"No," said Corvus. "Do you?"

I shook my head. "I can detect magic, but that's all."

"I don't think anyone is around that corner," said Corvus. "I would hear them otherwise."

"Really," I said. "Your hearing is that good?"

"At night, yes," said Corvus.

I frowned, working through the implications of that. Did that mean he could hear my heartbeat? Just as well that I had Cloaked when running from him at Niles Ringer's office, though I wondered if his senses were duller in the sunlight. Corvus struck me as a man who had a practical reason for everything that he did, and he wouldn't have worn those big sunglasses simply because he liked the way they looked. It was another piece of the puzzle. Maybe if I gathered together enough pieces I could figure out who he was…or what he was.

"Right," I said. "Let's put that to the test."

Corvus gestured, and I peered around the corner. The corridor continued, deserted as before, though I saw a metal door about fifty feet further down the hallway. The hallway ended in a concrete wall perhaps another sixty feet past the metal door.

"That door," I said. "Our best bet. We should have a look around."

"Agreed," said Corvus. "I think…wait."

He frowned and stooped, peering at the polished concrete floor. For a moment I thought he had dropped his wallet or something, but I didn't see anything. His head swiveled back and forth.

"What is it?" I said.

"Look at that," said Corvus, pointing at the floor. "What does that look like to you?"

I shrugged. "It doesn't look like anything. I think…"

I fell silent as I saw what he had noticed. There were scratches on the concrete, lots and lots of scratches. At first I thought that they had been left by wheels, by a pallet jack or a forklift or something, but they were too long and slender for that.

"You see?" said Corvus. "What does it look like to you?"

"Like…claw marks," I said. "Like something with claws was running through the hallway." I frowned. "Does McCade have animals? Like, a private zoo, or a kennel or something?" It seemed exceedingly odd for a rich man to build himself a secret zoo inside his mansion, but I had seen weirder things tonight.

"A kennel?" murmured Corvus. "Maybe. But they would be big dogs. Look at how far apart the clusters of scratches are."

I shrugged. "So?"

"I see you are a city girl," he said with just a hint of amusement.

I let out an exasperated sound. "There's nothing valuable to steal in the countryside. Stop being all clever and mysterious and tell me what the problem is."

"Those claw marks," said Corvus, spreading the fingers of his right hand. "Look at how far apart they are. Something with big paws made them. Something big and heavy." He scraped his shoe against the floor. "This kind of concrete doesn't scratch easily…"

"Then a really big dog?" I said. "Or…maybe a bear? He has a bear back here?" That seemed weird. I suppose a hungry bear might make a decent security measure, but locks and cameras would be less likely to eat their owner.

"I hope so," said Corvus.

I blinked. "Why? What's the alternative that makes a bear seems like the better possibility?"

"Are you familiar with summoning spells?" said Corvus.

"McCade has been trying to summon creatures from the Shadowlands?" I said. "That's illegal. Like, get-beheaded-on-Punishment-Day-illegal. It doesn't matter if he's friends with the Duke, the Inquisition would kill him for that."

"Half the things we have seen here tonight have been illegal," said Corvus, "and if my suspicions about his book are correct…no matter. Further speculation gains us nothing. I suggest we press onward, but with caution. If there is a wild animal back here, or some creature from the Shadowlands, we will need to be on our guard."

I nodded, and we walked in silence down the hall and stopped before the steel door. It was an impressive, solid security door, designed to keep intruders out…or wild animals within. There were no cameras over the door, and I cast the spell to detect magic. Again I felt the same buzzing auras of power I had sensed earlier, but there were no wards or magical alarms upon the door.

"Say," I said. "Since you apparently have good ears, can you hear anything behind that door?"

Corvus nodded and leaned against the door for a moment. "Some machinery. A large refrigerator or a freezer unit, I believe. Nothing else."

Another thought came to me. "You can cast spells, right? How good are you with the spell to detect magic?"

Corvus grimaced. "I am not particularly proficient with it. I can detect auras, and discern their natures, but I cannot focus the spell more than that."

"Ah, well," I said. "I suppose the only way we'll find out what's behind that door is by opening it."

"Profound," said Corvus. "Perhaps you could write greeting cards."

I looked at him. He kept a straight face.

"You're not as funny as you think you are," I said, and turned my attention to the door as I cast another spell. It was complex and demanded a great deal of focus, merging earth magic with psychokinetic force. I held my concentration, focusing the spell, and the door's lock released with a click.

"Impressive," said Corvus.

"Thanks," I said. I reached into my bag and pulled out a pair of black gloves, since we had reached the point where I didn't want to leave any fingerprints. Corvus followed suit, drawing the gloves from the pockets of his coat, and I pushed the door open.

The faint smell of rotting meat came to my nostrils at once.

I found myself in a large industrial kitchen. A row of stoves and ovens covered one wall, next to the humming walk-in freezer Corvus had overheard. A counter ran the length of the room, and an overflowing trash can stood next to the counter, generating the foul smell. In the opposite wall stood four niches the size of large closets, all of them sealed with sturdy steel bars. It looked like a row of prison cells, or…

Or exhibits at a zoo.

"Weird," I muttered.

"Truly," said Corvus.

I shook my head and took a few steps into the room, examining the trash can. It was full of white foam trays, the kind that grocery stores used to hold cuts of steak and pork. Likely the smell came from various bits of raw meat that had fallen into the can. I crossed to the stoves and pulled one of the ovens open. A thin layer of dust covered the burners, and the interior of the oven looked pretty clean. I had spent the last several weeks helping to clean the ovens at Duncan Catering Company's kitchen, so I knew what a well-used oven looked like, and this wasn't it.

"I don't think these have been used for a long time," I said.

"No," said Corvus. "Whatever was in those cages preferred to eat raw meat."

"Right," I said "So. Why are the cages empty now?"

Corvus shrugged. "Maybe McCade let them circulate among the guests."

"Wouldn't a thing that eats raw meat be a little obvious in a room full of rich jerks and Homeland Security officers?" I said.

Corvus shrugged again. "They're predators. I assume another kind of predator would fit right in."

"I can't tell if that was a joke or not," I said. There was another steel door at the far end of the. I cast the spell to sense the presence of magic again. There were no spells or magical traps upon the door, but the auras of power I had sensed before felt closer. "Whatever magical items McCade has hidden away are close. We should..."

Corvus took three quick steps back.

I spun. "What is it? Is..."

A sheet of white mist rolled across the floor, splitting into two separate flows. I feared that we had triggered some kind of trap, that poison gas was pouring into the kitchen. Except gas didn't act like that. The stream of mist split into two columns that seemed to thicken and harden and solidify. It was a bit like watching winter sleet condense into ice.

"Brace yourself," said Corvus. "Do you have any weapons?"

"Weapons?" I said. "No. Why? What's..."

The mist vanished, and it its place appeared...

I blinked.

Two creatures out of a nightmare appeared in the place of the mist.

They looked vaguely like wolves, albeit larger and far more muscular than normal wolves. Strange bony armor covered their long bodies and their heads, making it look as if they wore a second skeleton over their hides. Their fur was ragged and stringy, and their eyes burned with a peculiar intelligence.

"Wraithwolves," I said. "Goddamn it, he summoned wraithwolves."

I had never seen a wraithwolf before, but I knew what they were. The creatures were things of the Shadowlands, the strange parallel realm that connected the worlds, the home to the Warded Ways that the High Queen and her Elven nobles had used to leave their homeworld and reach Earth. When the High Queen's human armies fought against her various enemies in the misty realms of the Shadowlands, the wraithwolves prowled after the carnage of the battlefield, feasting upon the wounded and the stragglers.

James sometimes told me about the things he had seen in the battles of the Shadowlands. But he had only told me of the wraithwolves once during one of our late-night cigarettes, how they had had hunted him after he had taken his leg wound, how he had barely escaped. After telling that story he had smoked four cigarettes and gone to bed, and he had never spoken of the wraithwolves again. I don't think he had even told Lucy that story.

Seeing the wraithwolves up close, their rank, rotting smell filling my nostrils, their glowing eyes digging into me, I understood why James never wanted to speak of them.

"Have you ever fought a wraithwolf?" murmured Corvus in a quiet voice. The wraithwolf to my left looked him, its eyes unblinking.

"Never even seen them," I said. "Heard of them, though. They're going to kill us, aren't they?"

"They'll try," he said. "McCade must have summoned them and bound them as guardians. They're from the Shadowlands, so bullets won't hurt them."

"I don't have a gun," I said. I wondered why the wraithwolves hadn't attacked yet.

"Neither do I," said Corvus, opening and closing his right fist. "We need…"

The creatures shot forward in a blur. Corvus thrust out his left hand, and a brilliant ball of crackling blue-white lightning shot from his palm and struck the nearest wraithwolf in the chest. The creature rocked back with a tearing howl of pain as fingers of lightning stabbed up and down its limbs.

The second wraithwolf pivoted towards me, every muscle tensing as it prepared to spring. I didn't have any weapons. I didn't have any spells with the power of the lightning globe Corvus had just cast into the other wraithwolf.

But I could Cloak, so I did that instead.

I had the distinct pleasure of seeing the wraithwolf come to a halt, something like confusion come over its hideous face. The creature's eyes jerked back and forth, its nostrils flaring as it tried to pick up my scent, but the Cloak would baffle its sense of smell.

It hesitated for an instant, and then wheeled, springing towards Corvus in a smooth arc. I couldn't warn him, couldn't even move without releasing my Cloak. Fortunately, Corvus had no need of any warning. He dodged the wraithwolf's lunge, looking as calm and relaxed as he had upon the dance floor, but his eyes had turned solid black again.

He flicked his right wrist, his fingers opening…and suddenly a sword appeared in his hand.

At least, it resembled a sword. If shadows could have been collected and gathered into a blade, they would have looked like the weapon that Corvus had called into existence. It was a shaft of utter darkness that extended three feet from his hand, its edges flickering and gauzy. Even as the wraithwolf turned, Corvus wheeled, slashing the sword of shadows across the creature's flank. The dark sword parted hide and muscle as easily as if they had been paper, and the wraithwolf staggered with a scream of pain. Corvus brought the sword down, and his next stroke severed the wraithwolf's head, its black blood spurting across the concrete floor.

He started to straighten up, his eyes still filled with shadow, and the second wraithwolf slammed into him. Its weight drove him to the floor, its forepaws raking at his chest, its jaws clamped around his right forearm. Corvus couldn't get his sword arm free to strike, and he couldn't cast a spell of lightning at the creature, since the power would conduct through both of them.

A cold voice in my head pointed out that the time had come to abandon him.

If I fled now, the wraithwolf would kill him. Likely the creature would be too busy devouring his corpse to pursue me. If I was quick, I could enter McCade's inner sanctum, make off with the tablet, and escape before the wraithwolf finished its meal. If Corvus had been planning to betray me, his death would tie off that loose end nicely. For that matter, if I tried to help him, the wraithwolf might kill me, and if I died Russell would die. Russell's life mattered far more than Corvus's.

All this flashed through my mind in a heartbeat.

I prepared to sprint for the door on the far end of the kitchen…and I couldn't.

I just couldn't.

To this day I am not entirely sure why. It wasn't a pang of conscience – I didn't really have much of one left. Maybe I feared that Russell would one day learn all the illegal things I had done to save his life, and I didn't want to add leaving a man to die to the list.

Hell. Maybe I'm just an idiot.

I released my Cloak and began another spell, thrusting my hands towards the wraithwolf perched atop Corvus. My magical education had been very specific, with Morvilind focusing on spells he thought I might need as a thief and a general outline of magical theory. He had not given me much training in the elemental forms of magic, and very little in the way of battle spells. Likely he didn't want to arm me with any spells I might use against him, though compared to his magical power, I was a candle flame next to his inferno.

That said, he had taught me the basics, and I called elemental fire.

It was a simple spell, but I couldn't control it well. Someone like Morvilind or a veteran wizard of the Legion could have unleashed a tight sphere of flame that would have shot through the wraithwolf's skull like a superheated bullet. I only managed a cone of fire that washed over the wraithwolf's hindquarters. The beast reared back with a startled yip of pain and surprise, and for an absurd moment it sounded like a startled puppy.

The resemblance to a puppy vanished when the wraithwolf whirled to face me, its eyes ablaze with fury. The thing was going to tear me apart. I was a lot smaller than Corvus, and it could bite my head off with one twist of those massive jaws.

The beast started to spring, and I Cloaked again. The wraithwolf stumbled, head jerking back and forth as it tried to find me, and in that moment of hesitation Corvus rolled to one knee and brought his sword down. The blade sliced into the wraithwolf's neck, and the beast went into a spastic, jerking dance. I dropped my Cloak and dodged as the wraithwolf staggered past me, slammed into the side of the counter, and went limp, black slime pooling beneath it.

I let out a long breath and looked at Corvus.

"Damned things," muttered Corvus. His white dress shirt had been shredded and stained with blood. "Always hated them. Almost as bad as anthrophages. I..."

He wobbled a bit, the black sword vanishing, and had to put one hand on the nearby freezer to stay upright. I moved closer, peering at his wounds. Trying to save his life might have been a wasted effort. Depending on how badly the wraithwolf had bitten him, he might bleed out right now. If I escaped with the tablet, leaving behind a mauled corpse would definitely complicate things...

As I stepped closer to Corvus, his black eyes fell upon me like a physical weight, and I noticed three things at once.

First, with his shirt shredded, I saw his chest and stomach, and he was...well, let's just say he was impressively muscled. There was a reason that tuxedo fit him so well. If he ever wanted female attention, he could just take his shirt off and walk about in a confident manner.

Second, he had scars. A lot of scars. Sword scars, and other scars that looked like claw marks. The livid red gashes from the wraithwolf's claws formed cross-hatches with his old scars. One scar on his belly, just below his ribs, looked as if it had been made by a large-caliber bullet, and I suspected it had left a nasty exit wound in his back.

But the scars and the muscles were not at the forefront of my attention.

His tattoos were.

Specifically, his moving tattoos.

Spiraling black lines marked his torso and stomach, and as I watched the tattoos moved, writhing and flowing over his skin like...like...

Like shadows.

I looked at the blackness that filled his eyes, as if they had become spheres made of shadow.

I looked at his right hand, and saw the lines of black tattoos retreating from his wrist and up his damaged forearm. I knew then, with utter certainty, that when he had called that dark sword into existence, the tattoos had flowed up his arm and coalesced into his hand to form the sword.

And that meant...

A wave of fear rolled through me, more intense than any I had felt since beginning this enterprise.

"Oh, hell," I whispered. "You're a Shadow Hunter."

Oh, God. I had kissed a Shadow Hunter. If I died in the next few minutes, they could inscribe "NADIA MORAN, IDIOT" upon my tombstone.

"See?" said Corvus, his voice a hard rasp. "Told you I wasn't a vampire."

"Think I would have preferred that," I said. "You're an assassin."

"No," said Corvus. "No. I am not. We are executioners, not assassins."

"Oh, there's a fine distinction," I said, my mind racing.

I knew about the Shadow Hunters. Everyone did. They were a legendary organization of assassins, and according to the stories, they gained superhuman powers from symbiosis with a Shadowmorph, a creature of some kind from the Shadowlands. The Shadow Hunters turned up in a lot of movies and books, though the Inquisition always made sure the fictional Shadow Hunters killed traitors to the High Queen, Rebels, and corrupt businessmen. I had asked Morvilind once if the Shadow Hunters were real, and he had answered that if I valued my life, I would make sure to stay well away from the Shadow Hunters.

"It is," said Corvus, taking deep breaths. "We are not assassins. We only kill those who have earned execution."

"And you feed on them," I said. According to the tales, a Shadowmorph drank the life of its victims, transferring that power back to its host.

"Yes," said Corvus, and his shadow-filled eyes opened again. "Please do not stand so close to me just now. You are young and pretty and I'm…a bit hungry at the moment."

I took several hasty steps back, my eyes fixed on him.

"Hungry," I said. "Goddamn it. A Shadow Hunter."

"And what about you?" said Corvus, wincing as he closed his eyes.

"What about me?" I said. "I'm not a Shadow Hunter."

"Are you a half-elf?" said Corvus. His eyes darted back and forth behind closed lids, the black lines of the Shadowmorph skittering over his skin. "Or are you an Elven noble in disguise?"

"What are you talking about?" I said. "I'm not an Elf, and my mother didn't sleep with one."

"You cast an illusion spell," said Corvus. "A…Cloak spell, I believe it is called. You vanished so thoroughly that not even the Shadowmorph could sense you. Humans are forbidden to learn illusion magic, and the Inquisition kills any Elves that teach illusion or mind magic to humans. So what are you?"

That put an idea into my head. Maybe I could report Morvilind to the Inquisition for teaching me illusion magic. Of course, if I did that, he would use the vial of heart's blood to kill me. If he killed me before he cured

Russell, then the frostfever would kill Russell. A wave of bitter anger went through me. Morvilind didn't need chains or brands or drugs to control me the way McCade controlled his borrowed slaves. He had built a perfect box around me, a box from which I could not escape.

Though the wounded Shadow Hunter in front of me was a bit more dangerous at the moment.

"What I am," I said, "is concerned that you're going to bleed to death unless you get something on those cuts." The gashes across his chest and stomach were bad enough. His right forearm was a mangled mess beneath the torn sleeve of his coat. Unless he saw a doctor or a wizard with a powerful Healing spell within the next few hours, he was probably going to lose the arm. Or die of blood loss.

"No," said Corvus, shaking his head. "Just keep watch for a moment, will you?"

"Fine," I said. "I'll stand here and watch you bleed to death."

"You won't," said Corvus, rolling his shoulders. The movement had to pain him…but then I saw something astonishing.

His wounds were shrinking. The lines of the peculiar black tattoo writhed and twisted over them, making the gashes shrink centimeter by centimeter. As I watched, they closed, becoming livid red marks, then scars, and then vanishing entirely. Within five minutes, the wounds were gone. Corvus let out a ragged sigh and opened his eyes, which had returned to their normal brown color. He looked somehow…sharper, harder, hungrier, and I had the distinct feeling that he was undressing me with his eyes.

I watched him, ready to cast a spell if he tried anything.

Instead he looked at the bloodstained tatters of his shirt and coat and shook his head.

"Pity it's a rented tuxedo," I said. "You're not getting the deposit back."

"No," he said.

I licked my lips, pushing moisture into my dry mouth. "Are we going to have to fight?"

He blinked in surprise. "Why would we do that?"

"Because that Shadowmorph just expended a lot of power to heal you," I said. "Because a Shadowmorph feeds of life energy, and it's probably real hungry after all that exercise. Because I'm the nearest source of life energy."

He shook his head. "I will not kill you or harm you, unless in self-defense. I do not have a decree of execution for your life. The law of the Shadow Hunters forbids it."

"The law?" I scoffed. "Since when do people follow the law? I'm sure you're just like the Elven nobles and their pets, mouthing about the law in public and then screwing a drugged slave when you…"

He slammed his left hand onto the metal counter with enough force to leave a dent, and I flinched back.

"I keep my word and follow the law of the Shadow Hunters, Katerina Annovich," said Corvus, his voice as cold and hard as the dented steel counter, "at a cost you cannot begin to imagine. I have kept my word and followed the law for decades before you were born. I will violate neither now."

Silence stretched between us. A dozen smart remarks started and died on my lips.

"Um," I said. "Okay, then."

"Thank you for my life," Corvus said, lifting his hand from the dented counter.

"You were doing pretty well on your own," I said.

"I might have," said Corvus, "since I was about to shift the sword to my left hand. Or the wraithwolf might have ripped my head off. I am stronger than most men, but that matters little in hand-to-hand combat with a creature like a wraithwolf. Had I known McCade had such guardians, I would have come better prepared."

"You did pretty well on your own," I said again. "Better than I would have. One of those things would have torn me to pieces. Two…" I would not have lasted more than a few seconds. "Thank you for killing them. I would have run."

"Or hidden with that Cloak spell," said Corvus. "That was how you got away from me in the alley, wasn't it? You Cloaked yourself and waited until I left."

"If you had waited a little longer, you would have found me," I said. "That spell is exhausting, and I was almost at the end of my stamina when you left."

"I see," said Corvus, nodding the way a man does when a vexing mystery has been solved at last. "I thought you had gone into one of the offices, but I couldn't hear you running. The Shadowmorph is less potent in the daylight, but I still should have been able to hear you."

"Not while Cloaked," I said.

"No," said Corvus. "Not while Cloaked. The prospect that you might have employed an Elven spell of illusion escaped me entirely. I shall not make that mistake again."

"What were you doing there, anyway?" I said.

"The same thing you were, I imagine," said Corvus. "I hired the services of a man named Niles Ringer to forge an invitation to the gala."

"He probably overcharged you."

"Egregiously," said Corvus, "but the invitation was effective. We are both here, are we not?"

"That we are," I said. "We are going next?"

"Onward," said Corvus. "We both have our missions."

"And what is yours? Are you here to assassinate," Corvus frowned, and I rolled my eyes, "are you here to…to execute McCade? You have one of these decrees of execution?"

"A conditional one," said Corvus. "Only if he possesses a specific book."

"And what is this book," I said, "that it should earn a death sentence from a Shadow Hunter?"

"Nothing you should know about," said Corvus.

"I already know illusion magic," I said. "That's a death sentence right there. What's another one atop it?"

"No," said Corvus. "No, some knowledge you are better off never possessing. Even the mere possession of this knowledge can harm you. If we enter this inner sanctum and do not find the book, that is that. Better that you never know what I thought to find here."

I made a show of rolling my eyes, but a thread of dark suspicion went through my mind. What if this book was some means of killing me? Another part of my mind pointed out the ridiculousness of that thought. If Corvus wanted to kill me, he could have let the wraithwolves do it.

Or he could have summoned his dark sword and feasted upon me once the wraithwolves were slain. He looked harder, sharper, than he had a few moments earlier, and I knew his Shadowmorph was hungry. I could feel its presence brushing against my thoughts, a dark aura that called to me…and I admitted I found it attractive, the way his kiss had been.

Better avoid that thought entirely.

"Fine," I said. "Let's keep going. The sooner we get out of here, the better."

"Agreed," said Corvus, and I started for the door on the far side of the kitchen.

Another grim thought occurred to me. "Do you think McCade will know that the wraithwolves have been killed? If he summoned them, he might be linked to them."

"Perhaps," said Corvus. "I am more curious why he let them loose during his party."

"Guard dogs?" I said. "Big, nasty, guard dogs?" I checked the door. It wasn't warded, but it was locked, and I took a deep breath to clear my buzzing mind. I had cast a lot of spells tonight, and the effort was starting to wear me down. "Or maybe he wanted to dispose of someone. The wraithwolves would eat all the meat, and he could dump the bones down that big garbage disposal in the sink."

"The first possibility is more likely," said Corvus. "I speak from experience when I say that a party is not the best venue to kill someone."

"Then what are you doing here?"

He only snorted in answer.

I focused and again cast the spell to undo a lock. The door clicked, and I swung it open. A narrow utility corridor stretched beyond it, lit only by a pair of light bulbs, and then opened into a large mechanical room. I supposed it would be amusing if I had come all this way only to break into McCade's furnace room. On the other hand, the magical auras I had sensed had been in this direction, which made me wonder if McCade stored magical relics in his furnace room.

It was a large place, at least as large as the room with the slaves, though air handlers and rows of transformers filled much of the space. The machinery gave off a constant wheeze, and sometimes a rattling cough came from one of the air handlers. A layer of dust and grit covered the floor, likely left over from the original construction, and rasped against the soles of my shoes.

In the far wall stood a vault door, an eight-foot slab of steel adorned with multiple locks and bars. To judge from the reinforced frame, it was at least eight inches thick, and strong enough to resist gunfire, dynamite, and maybe even a small bulldozer. I couldn't see any electronic alarms, but I suspected they were there.

"Can you get through that?" said Corvus.

"Yep," I said, casting the spell to sense magic. There were no spells or wards upon the vault door. "I've gotten through harder doors. It'll take me a minute or two, though." It would take multiple castings to get through the locks and the alarms, and I was tired enough already. "It's your turn to keep watch."

"Of course," said Corvus. "I…"

He spun, the Shadowmorph sword appearing in his right hand once more.

"What is it?" I said, wishing I had thought of a way to smuggle a gun into the mansion. "Is…"

Two rivers of mist flowed across the floor of the utility room.

"More wraithwolves," I said. "There were four cages in the kitchen."

"I will stun one," said Corvus, and lightning crackled in his free hand. "Use your Cloak to distract the other. I will dispatch it, and then kill the second before it can recover from the lightning."

That was an awfully tenuous plan, especially when we both were already weakened. The rivers of mist split, solidifying and hardening as they did so.

This time we found ourselves facing six wraithwolves, not two.

"Well," I said, my heart hammering with sudden terror, "guess McCade kept them two to a cage."

"Could you Cloak both of us at once?" said Corvus. He whipped his shadow-sword in a wide arc, and the misshapen creatures cringed back to avoid it. If all the wraithwolves charged at once, they could bury both of us with ease.

That would not be a pleasant death.

"Maybe. Probably," I said. "I couldn't hold it for very long. Not long enough for them to get bored and wander off."

One of the wraithwolves inched forward, and Corvus thrust, the beast jumping back. Sooner or later they would work up the nerve to charge. Or they would sit here and guard us until McCade and his security guards arrived to shoot us. We were trapped with no way out.

Unless…

My fear turned into something far sharper.

There was another spell Morvilind had taught me, one that I had used several times. Every single time it had almost gotten me killed, but "almost killed" was better than "definitely killed", and if I stayed here, I would definitely be killed.

I stooped, grabbed a handful of dust and a chip of concrete from the floor, and whirled to face the vault door.

"What are you doing?" said Corvus.

"Keep them off me," I said, summoning magical power as I concentrated. I hoped I had enough strength left to work the spell. "Just for a few seconds."

Silver light whirled and flared around my hands, a sheet of gray mist rippling over the vault door. The strain was immense, but I gritted my teeth and forced myself to keep working the spell.

One of the wraithwolves snarled, and I heard a thunderclap and saw a flash of blue-white light as Corvus flung a globe of lightning. A chorus of snarls rose from behind me, claws scraping against the floor as the wraithwolves braced themselves to spring.

In that moment, gray light washed over me, and the curtain of mist seemed to become deeper somehow…and through the mist I glimpsed a forest of barren, dead trees, a cold wind blowing over my face and tugging at my skirt and hair.

The rift way was open.

"Now!" I shouted. "Jump! Go!"

Corvus whirled and ran past me as the wraithwolves sprang, and I jumped after him. I should have hit the steel vault door and bounced off.

Instead I fell through the mist, and into the dead forest beyond.

The gate had taken me to the Shadowlands, to the haunted places between the worlds.

CHAPTER 8
SHADOWLANDS

I hit the ground, pale grasses rustling beneath me, rolled to one knee, and turned to face my gate. I saw the mechanical room back in McCade's mansion, the wraithwolves racing after us, and with an effort of will I dismissed the spell.

The rift way flared and disappeared, and I saw that we were in a clearing, dead trees ringing us, pale grasses everywhere, the starless, black sky writhing with ghostly ribbons of blue and green and purple fire.

Right about then I passed out.

If you've ever had heatstroke, or moderate dehydration, magical exhaustion is something like that. The blood pressure drops, and it's usually accompanied by a sudden sweat and a loud humming noise in the ears. I managed to take two steps towards the dead trees. Corvus said something, and my vision turned gray, and then white, and I just had the wits to get to my knees before I keeled over.

I wasn't out long.

My vision swam back into focus, and I sat up with a startled curse. Corvus stood nearby, the Shadowmorph sword in his right hand, his eyes darting back and forth. Belatedly I realized that the smell of his bloody clothes might draw all manner of predators. We had to get out of here as soon as possible.

"Oh, hell," I said. "Did I drop it? Tell me I didn't drop it."

"Dropped what?" said Corvus.

If I had dropped it, we were in a lot of trouble.

But I hadn't. The concrete chip and the dust were still gripped in the fingers of my left hand. A little relief went through me. That, at least, was one less thing I had to worry about.

Though there were plenty of worries left behind.

"Our way back," I said, trying to get my legs underneath me.

Corvus held out a hand. I looked at it for a moment, wondering at the wisdom of touching a Shadow Hunter. Then I shrugged and held out my free hand. He heaved me up without a hint of effort, and I staggered a little, but I managed not to fall on my face.

"A piece of concrete," said Corvus, incredulous. "You brought a piece of concrete with us?"

"I don't know why that surprises you so much," I said. "Given that I just opened a rift way to the Shadowlands in front of you."

"Another spell," said Corvus, "that humans are not supposed to know."

"Yeah," I said. "I had a good…well, he wasn't a good teacher. I had an interesting teacher, let's say." I rubbed my forehead with a moment with my free hand, trying to will my headache into acquiescence. It didn't work. "You've been here before?"

"I have," said Corvus, looking at the dead trees as the ribbons of ghostly light danced overhead, throwing strange shadows in all directions. "A long time ago, when I was a man-at-arms in service to an Elven lord."

"Before you became a Shadow Hunter, I take it," I said.

"Yes," murmured Corvus, still gazing into the trees. Then he shook his head, as if throwing off a dark memory, and turned to face me again. "We need to depart at once. There are darker creatures than wraithwolves in the Shadowlands."

I almost asked if that included Shadowmorphs, but for once in my life I managed to hold my tongue.

"Actually," I said, "we're going to avoid both of them. If we hurry up."

"And just how are we going to accomplish this?" said Corvus.

"How much do you know about the Shadowlands?" I said, rubbing the concrete chip.

"More than I would wish," said Corvus. "This is the realm that connects the worlds. The Warded Ways cross through the Shadowlands, and are the closest things to safe paths. Many dangerous creatures dwell here, some more alien than you can imagine. Parts of the Shadowlands are claimed as demesnes by powerful lords, whether by spirits or mortal wizards, but such lords cannot leave their demesnes." He looked at the dead trees for a moment. "Unless I miss my guess, we are in the demesne of the Knight of Grayhold, a lord who controls a large portion of the Shadowlands nearest to Earth."

"Entirely correct," I said. "Missing only one part." Morvilind's old lessons filtered through my head. "Every mortal world casts a shadow into the Shadowlands. The Elves call it an umbra. The umbra touches the material world in different places. So if you do it right, you can open a rift way to the Shadowlands, cross through a few miles in the umbra, open a rift way back, and cross over several thousand miles of the real world with only a few minutes' journey in the Shadowlands."

"Indeed?" said Corvus. "I never knew that."

"It's a secret among the Elven nobles and wizards," I said.

"So if it is possible to journey over thousands of miles with a few moments' travel in the Shadowlands," said Corvus, "why do not more of the Elven lords travel in such a manner?"

"Two reasons," I said. "Wait, three. One, it doesn't work in a heavily warded destination. It's easy to block a rift way from the Shadowlands with a few spells. Two, sometimes the distance isn't a few miles. Sometimes it's hundreds and hundreds of miles, and it has to be on foot. Gunpowder doesn't ignite and gasoline doesn't burn in the Shadowlands. Electronics don't work, either." Belatedly I remembered that I had forgotten to turn off my burner phone. Well, it was a useless brick now. "Third…the Shadowlands are dangerous. Even for Elven archmages. It's safer to fly or drive three thousand miles on Earth than it is to walk three miles in the Shadowlands."

"I am keenly aware of that last fact," said Corvus. Perhaps he had acquired some of his previous scars in the Shadowlands. "Then you have abandoned your mission? You plan to escape from McCade's mansion entirely?"

"Nope," I said. "We're going to go right back where we were…but maybe a dozen yards or so further to the right."

Corvus blinked, and then I saw him figure it out. "You will open the rift way back to Earth within the vault door."

"That's right," I said. "Another fun fact about the Shadowlands." I hefted the concrete chip. "You can use physical objects from a specific location like…oh, a compass, I suppose. It will draw us to the place in the umbra of Earth that corresponds to an actual physical location on Earth. Then all I have to do is put a little more power into the spell, and the rift way will open inside McCade's vault."

"Admirably clever," said Corvus. "I suggest we proceed before something finds us. The wraithwolves are powerful and fast, and they are nonetheless some of the weaker creatures of the Shadowlands."

"Agreed," I said. Of all the many ways I could die doing Morvilind's dirty work, getting eaten alive by some horror out of the Shadowlands would be one of the worst. I took a deep breath and summoned magic. It came easier, far easier than it would have in the real world. All magic originated from the Shadowlands, and it was the source of the power that leeched into the real world that I could touch and use. Until the High Queen had breached Earth's umbra and allowed the aura of the

Shadowlands to spill through, magic had been unknown on Earth…

I blinked.

No, that wasn't quite right. There had been magic on Earth before the Conquest, hadn't there? Else how had the Assyrians enchanted that tablet that Morvilind wanted so badly?

It was a question for another time.

I forced the magic through a spell and gestured with my free hand, and the chip of concrete began to shimmer with a ghostly gray glow. I turned it back and forth, feeling the tugging of the spell against my thoughts.

"This way," I decided, pointing into the dead trees. I tried to discern out the direction, and then realized that since the Shadowlands had neither sun nor moon nor stars, there was no such thing as north or south or east or west here. "About three miles, I think. Then I can open a rift way back to McCade's vault…"

A hideous, shrieking cry rang out from the trees behind us. Corvus whirled with catlike grace, his dark sword coming up, his face tight and hard. The echoes from the cries died away…and a dozen more answered.

A dozen cries that were coming closer.

"Um," I said. "What is that?"

"Anthrophages," said Corvus. "An entire pack."

"Anthrophages?" I said. "What is an anthrophage?" It didn't sound pleasant.

"They're ghouls," said Corvus. "Essentially. No one know what they really are. They feast on living flesh when they can get it, but they have no qualms about eating the dead. They attack and kill anyone they can catch in the Shadowlands, and haunt the battlefields."

"They sound like wraithwolves," I said.

"They're worse than wraithwolves," said Corvus. "Not as strong, but faster and much smarter." Again that chilling chorus of screams rose from the dead trees. "They hunt by scent."

"Oh," I said. "The blood in your clothes…"

Corvus shook his head. "They could hunt you by the smell of your sweat. A rift way. Can you open it here?"

"I could," I said, "but I have no idea where it would go. We might end up in the middle of the Sahara. Or in the center of the Pacific."

"Your Cloaking spell," said Corvus. "Could you cast it over both of us?"

"In the Shadowlands, yes," I said, "but I don't know how long I could hold it."

"Then do so," said Corvus. "Quickly!"

I started to snap that he couldn't give me orders, but the grim urgency in his face made the retort die in my throat. I wouldn't say he was afraid, not precisely…but he was certain that if we did not get away from the anthrophages, we were going to die. After seeing his capabilities, after seeing him handle himself in the fight against the wraithwolves, I knew that if something alarmed him, I had better take notice.

"Fine," I said. "Hold still." I stepped next to him and grabbed his elbow. "Whatever you do, don't move. I can't maintain the Cloak if you move. And stay in contact with me. If you stop touching me, the Cloak stops shielding you and the anthrophages find you."

In answer he slipped out of my grasp and put his arm around my shoulder.

Well, that would work too.

I summoned magic and cast the spell, silver light flashing around my fingers as we vanished. Back on Earth, summoning enough power to Cloak both of us at once would have been hard. Here, it was far easier, but concentrating to keep the spell in place was just as challenging. It was a difficult task, and I gritted my teeth, focusing the way I did when lifting a particularly heavy barbell or sprinting the final mile of a long run.

A moment later the anthrophages burst from the dead trees, loping over the dusty ground.

They looked vaguely man-shaped, tall and thin and skeletal. Ropy muscles moved beneath their glistening gray hides, and some of them ran on two legs, but others ran on all fours. Jagged black claws jutted from their fingers and toes, and their eyes were venomous pits of yellow. They did not have noses, only triangular pits in the center of their faces, yet they seemed able to hunt by scent. They spread out through the clearing, lowering their grotesque faces to the ground and sniffing. As they bent over, I saw that their ears were long and pointed, that a row of black spikes jutted from their spines. The stench of them, a mixture of rotting meat and sulfur, washed over me, and I tried to keep from gagging.

I held the Cloak as the anthrophages moved back and forth, snarling at each other in some sort of mewling, growling language. Sweat trickled down my back, a faint quiver of fatigue going through my limbs. The Cloak spell blocked scent as well as sight and sound, so I didn't have to worry about the creatures sniffing us out. I did worry that they were going to walk into us. The Cloak made us undetectable, but that would not keep an anthrophage from blundering into us through dumb luck.

The trembling in my legs got worse. I took deep, long breaths, trying to relax my legs, and Corvus's iron-hard fingers settled in a gentle but firm grip around my right shoulder. That actually helped me stay standing, and I poured all my concentration into the Cloak, keeping the spell in place. Sooner or later the anthrophages would give up and go in pursuit of other prey.

But they didn't.

The creatures kept moving back and forth through the clearing, and I realized they were searching in a systematic fashion. If the anthrophages hunted through scent, then they had not found any trail leading from the clearing. Eventually, I knew, they would give up…but they would find us before that.

A shudder went through me as I fought to maintain the Cloak. I had to open a rift way back to Earth. Better to take the chance of appearing at some random location than to say here to be devoured. Except to open the rift way I would have to release the Cloak, and it would take me a few moments to draw in the necessary magical power. There was no way Corvus could hold off the anthrophages long enough for me to gather the spell.

To sum up our situation in a word, we were screwed.

My trembling got worse, the effort of holding the Cloak harder. An anthrophage moved closer to us, sniffing at the dusty ground. The thing was following our trail, smelling the path of Corvus's blood and my sweat. It would walk right into us, and then we would be dead. I felt Corvus tense as he prepared to move…

Then the anthrophages stopped.

In perfect unison, all of the creatures turned their heads to look in the same direction. I couldn't see anything, but all the anthrophages were staring at something. They went as motionless as statues.

Then they raced away as one, vanishing into the dead trees.

A moment later we were alone in the clearing.

I held the Cloak as long as I could, maybe another ninety seconds. Then my entire body shuddered, and only Corvus's arm kept me from pitching over. The Cloaking spell unraveled and we reappeared, my breath sounding loud and uneven in my ears. I feared the anthrophages would return at once, that they had only hidden themselves to wait until we appeared, but nothing moved in the dead trees.

They were gone.

"Excellent work," said Corvus.

"Thanks," I muttered, blinking the sweat from my forehead. The beginnings of a massive headache stirred behind my eyes. If I lived through this, I was going to sit in a hot bath with a bottle of ibuprofen for hours. "Surprised that worked."

"Your skill with illusion magic is impressive," said Corvus. "But the Shadowlands are a dangerous place. Little wonder those who travel its reaches prefer to stay to the Warded Ways."

"Yep," I said, slipping out from under his arm. I didn't want to lean on him too much. His Shadowmorph was still hungry, and I was exhausted. His instincts would be screaming that he could feed upon me, and for all his talk of self-control, I trusted actions, not words. "Let's go before whatever scared off our new friends finds us."

"Perhaps they found likelier prey," said Corvus.

"They were screaming when they attacked us," I said. "Like hounds flushing out birds or something. They ran away from us in silence. Like they didn't want to be noticed."

"That is a very good point," said Corvus. "Lead the way."

I nodded, held up the glowing concrete chip, refreshed my sense of direction, and started walking.

We moved through the dead trees as quietly as we could. The trees were twisted and distorted, glowing moss clinging to their branches here and there. Morvilind had told me that each world's umbra was a twisted reflection of the world that cast it into the Shadowlands, that you could find distorted reflections of cities and mountains and even significant historical events in a world's umbra. Considering some of the things that had happened in human history, I hoped we didn't encounter any of those historical reflections.

Suddenly we came to another clearing, and I stopped.

"Damn it," I muttered.

A road of dull white stone stretched before us in either direction. It was about twenty feet wide, smooth and flat and hard. Alongside the road stood monoliths of rough gray stone, each of their four sides covered with glowing Elven hieroglyphics. The stones stood alongside the road at regular intervals, about every thirty yards or so.

"The Warded Ways," I said. The ward spells upon the monoliths kept off most of the predators of the Shadowlands, allowing travelers and armies to traverse the Shadowlands in…well, not safety, but at least somewhat less danger. The Warded Ways crisscrossed the Shadowlands, leading to the umbrae of dozens of different worlds.

"I remember this road," said Corvus, gazing at the ribbon of white stone with a distant expression. "This very road. I marched here as a man-at-arms, long ago. I…" He shook his head, his expression hardening again. "We should continue on…"

"No," I said. "We have a problem. We have to cross the road to reach our entry point."

Corvus shrugged. "So? At worst, we can shelter upon the road if the anthrophages return."

"No," I said. "The Inquisition will know if we stay upon the road for too long."

"They could not possibly know that," said Corvus.

"How do you think the High Queen knows when the Archons or the frost giants or someone else tries to open a rift way to Earth?" I said. "How do you think she knows when someone tries to attack? If someone stays on a Warded Way within Earth's umbra for too long, it alerts the wizards of the Inquisition, and the High Queen calls out some of her nobles to meet the attack."

"And how do you know that?" said Corvus.

"Same way I know illusion magic," I said. Morvilind had mentioned it, not out of any concern for my welfare, but to keep his secrets from falling into the grasp of the Inquisition should I find myself in the Shadowlands. "Someone taught me. We'll have to go around. Sometimes the Warded Ways cross over streams or ravines, and we can go under the bridge..."

"There isn't enough time," said Corvus.

I opened my mouth to answer, but he moved before I could speak. His arms coiled around me like steel bands, and for an awful moment I was sure that his self-control had snapped, that he was going to call his dark blade, drive it through my chest, and feast upon my life force. Instead he slung me over his shoulders in a fireman's carry, and did it so fast that I could not react.

Then he sprinted forward.

He could move fast, even when bearing my weight. Far faster than a normal man should have been able to go. The Shadowmorph must have been lending him strength. He sprinted forward, jumped, and landed maybe a third of the way across the Warding Way. He sprinted forward another few yards and jumped again. We shot through the air, and he landed on the dirt on the far side of the road, my chin bouncing off his side. Corvus stopped, turned, and put me back on my feet.

He wasn't even breathing very hard.

"Don't do that again," I said, wobbling a bit. God, but he was strong. He would have been strong even without the Shadowmorph's influence. I cast the spell to detect the presence of magic, and felt a faint stirring from the nearby monoliths. "It's activated, but…"

"But not very much," said Corvus. "The Inquisition, for all its power, does not have infinite resources. A dozen different major concerns continually occupy their attention, and wizards with the divinatory skill to see into the Shadowlands are not that common. Someone will investigate what we just did, I am sure…as soon as they can get around to it."

"Fine," I spat out. His logic made sense, I had to admit, but I still did not like it. "Then let's get the hell out of here before someone does come to investigate."

"Can you run?" he said. "Or should I carry you."

"Oh, shut up."

We jogged into the trees, following the pale light in my hand. The ground became rockier, more uneven, the trees more twisted. Here and there I saw piles of yellowing skulls stacked up like miniature pyramids. I didn't know if they were real skulls or some distorted reflection of the real world, and I didn't want to find out. The concrete chip in my hand glowed brighter, the mental tugging growing more insistent.

The trees thinned, and suddenly I found myself standing on the edge of a precipice, a vast canyon that had to be at least a half-mile deep and two miles wide. A turbulent river surged through the heart of the canyon, and it was so far down that I spotted clouds floating below me. We didn't have canyons like this on Earth. Maybe there were canyons like this on Mars, or this was some sort of abstract representation of a historical event.

"Here," I said. "It's here. This location corresponds to the vault in McCade's mansion. I can open the rift way from here."

"It's not over the edge, I hope?" said Corvus, glancing at the rocky ground far below.

I shook my head. "Right at the edge." I took deep breaths, clearing my aching, buzzing mind to summon the power I needed to push open the rift way back to Earth. As before, the magic came more easily, but the effort to control it was no less, and I was already tired.

"How long?" said Corvus.

"A few moments," I said. "Please shut up so I can concentrate."

Corvus snorted, but turned to watch the dead forest. I held out the concrete chip and the handful of dust, focusing my will and power upon them. The silvery glow around my hand grew brighter, and a curtain of mist rippled into existence, the air growing colder and colder against my bare arms.

Wait. It wasn't supposed to do that.

"Katerina!" snapped Corvus, his voice cracking like a whip. "Hurry!"

I frowned, looked over my shoulder, and was so shocked by what I saw that I almost lost my grip on the spell.

A…thing was floating towards us.

The wraithwolves had looked like twisted wolves. The anthrophages had looked vaguely human. This thing, this monster, whatever it was, had no analogues in the real world.

A huge sphere of glistening gray flesh floated overhead, black veins pulsing and throbbing in the slime-coated hide. From the underside of the sphere hung dozens of black tentacles, their sides covered in razor-edged barbs. A cluster of misshapen grayish-green flesh nodules adorned the bottom of the pulsing sphere, and dozens of fanged mouths dotted the nodules, opening and closing to reveal jagged fangs. Each mouth looked large enough to bite me in half.

I had seen a lot of terrifying things working for Morvilind, but this was in the top ten.

The thing was floating right towards me.

That put it in the top five. Maybe even the top three.

I whirled to face the rippling sheet of mist, throwing every last scrap of will and magic I could muster into it. The mist writhed, and then began to glow with pale gray light, shining brighter and brighter. Through the light and the mist I glimpsed a large room of black stone, and I was pretty sure it was McCade's vault on Earth.

"Corvus!" I shouted. "Go!"

I turned and saw him running at me. The huge creature floated after him, moving at least as fast as a car. I spun, took three running steps, and jumped over the edge of the vast chasm.

The rift way swallowed me.

CHAPTER 9
BOOKS AND SCROLLS

I hit a floor of black stone, rolled, and landed on my back with a groan. I sat up just as Corvus stumbled through the rift way, and beyond him I saw the huge spherical creature lowering itself toward the ground. It couldn't fit through the gate, but those tentacles could.

At once I released the spell, and the rift way snapped shut, the view of the Shadowlands and the ghastly horror vanishing.

I flopped upon the floor, breathing hard, and Corvus knelt next to me.

"Are you injured?" he said.

"No," I said, sitting up with a grunt. "Just tired. Ugh. What the hell was that thing?"

"I have no idea," said Corvus. "I have never encountered one before. I do not know if such creatures are native to the Shadowlands, or if it came from some distant world. The Shadowlands are supposedly infinite."

"Ugly thing," I said. I pushed off the floor, stood, and managed not to fall onto my face. "Just as well it didn't follow us. It wouldn't do to end McCade's gala with some alien monster rampaging through the guests."

"It would make for a memorable Conquest Day," said Corvus, his tone grim as he looked around.

"Hah," I said, and I looked around myself.

For a moment I was too baffled to speak.

I wasn't in a vault. I wasn't in a utility room or a mechanical room.

The room…it looked like I had landed in a temple of some kind.

For one thing, it was big, about the size of a mid-sized church, with a vaulted ceiling about thirty feet over my head. The walls and floor were built of gleaming black marble, and a dais rose at the far end of the rectangular room. There was even an altar and a gleaming golden symbol hanging on the wall above it.

"Looks like a church," I said.

"It's not," said Corvus, and his voice was harder than I had heard it yet. His dark sword returned to his right hand, and his eyes moved back and forth as if he expected attack from any direction. "Look closer."

I did…and I felt my frown deepen.

James and Lucy Marney's church had stained-glass windows depicting Jesus and the apostles preaching to crowds or tending sheep or doing various other religious things. This room, this temple, had lines of symbols marching up the walls of black marble, strange symbols of wedge-shaped lines that I recognized as cuneiform after a moment, cuneiform similar to that upon the tablet Morvilind wanted. There was an empty space on the dais before the altar, and I saw a double circle ringed with Elven hieroglyphs. Morvilind had not taught me any summoning spells, but I recognized a summoning circle when I saw one. The Marneys' church taught that the communion wine was the blood of Christ, but I was entirely certain the wine did not leave crusted bloodstains upon the altar, nor fill the air with a metallic, rotting reek as it dried.

And the golden symbol above the altar was not a cross.

It looked like a peculiarly stylized sunburst. No, that wasn't quite right. The nine rays coming off the central orb of the symbol were too wavy for that. Instead, the rays look liked…tentacles, tentacles that surrounded a fanged mouth.

"Definitely," I said, "not a church. Damn it. We're not on Earth, are we? I screwed up the rift way. We…"

"No," said Corvus. "Look." He pointed. A vault door stood in the wall behind me, identical to the one I had seen in McCade's mechanical room. It was the same door.

I summoned power and cast the spell to sense magic, and at once the sensations flooded over my mind. I felt the buzzing, snarling auras I had detected earlier, but much closer. They were here with me, now, in this very room. I also noticed a dark overtone in many of the auras, a nauseating and greasy sensation that made my skin crawl.

Dark magic.

That meant Morvilind had sent me to steal an object of dark magic.

"Oh, hell," I muttered.

"You recognize the symbol, then?" said Corvus.

"No," I said. "What is it?"

Corvus hesitated. "It is not something you should know."

"For God's sake," I said. "Today I've almost been killed by wraithwolves, anthrophages, and whatever that floating greasy tentacle thing was. What is worse than that?"

"This is," said Corvus. "It is the symbol of the Dark Ones."

"Dark Ones? That sounds downright ominous," I said. I didn't recognize the title. "What are they really called?"

"No one knows," said Corvus. "Save perhaps for their cultists. They are creatures that dwell in the realm beyond the Shadowlands, in the place called the Void."

"That's the source of dark magic," I said. "The High Queen forbids all traffic with or summoning from the Void."

"She does," said Corvus. "It was one of her disagreements with the Archons when they drove her from the Elven homeworld. There are cults among both Elves and humans that worship the Dark Ones and attempt to summon them up. The Dark Ones are incredibly dangerous, and attempting to summon one or even worshipping one is an automatic death sentence from the Inquisition."

"Then McCade is one of these cultists," I said.

"Perhaps even the high priest of his cult," said Corvus. "He built all this, or his father did, and he likely has followers."

"Does that earn him an automatic death sentence…ah, decree of execution from the Shadow Hunters?" I said.

Corvus's hard eyes turned towards me. "The Shadow Hunters are the enemies of the cultists of the Dark One."

"Right," I said. Well, the Inquisition might hate the cultists, but since I was pretty sure the bloodstains on that altar were human, the cultists did not seem like good guys. That said, I didn't care. I hadn't come here to hunt down crazy cultists who worshipped monsters from beyond the Void. I had come here to steal an enspelled tablet. "Let's see if we can find that book of yours. I suppose your decrees of execution are picky about the particulars."

"At this point," said Corvus, scowling at the golden sigil of the Dark Ones upon the wall, "it is a formality. This temple could not have been constructed without the knowledge of Paul McCade, and he must die. But the Silent Hunters adhere to our decrees."

"Stay away from that summoning circle," I said as we climbed the steps to the dais. "There's some kind of spell on it. I don't know what it will do, but I really don't want to find out."

"Nor do I," said Corvus, and we kept well away from the circle and its ring of Elven hieroglyphs. Standing too close to the circle made me dizzy, like I was standing atop a skyscraper and staring at the street far below. For a moment I had a vision of losing my balance, of falling into the circle, a fanged maw rising up to meet me…

"Katerina?" said Corvus.

I recognized the presence of a mental influence upon my thoughts. Whatever spell within in the circle was trying to call me to it.

"Definitely," I said, walking away, "stay well away from that circle."

I reached the altar. It was a massive slab of black marble, adorned on the sides with cuneiform symbols. I wondered how much McCade had spent upon black marble to adorn his weird little temple. Clearly the man had too much money. Bloodstains marked the front of the black marble, dull and dark, and the air smelled vaguely of rotting meat. A number of objects rested atop the altar – a golden chalice, a curved dagger, and an open book resting upon a pedestal.

"That your book?" I said. There was an alcove in the wall behind the altar. One side held a row of metal boxes for circuit breakers, likely for the electric lights shining in the temple's ceiling. The opposite side held a utility shelf containing a miscellaneous assortment of objects. There was a small leather pouch, and my eyes widened as I saw the gleam of gems. Perhaps McCade used those gems in his rituals to contact the Dark Ones.

I tucked the pouch into my duffel bag. It's not as if Morvilind pays me an allowance or a salary or anything.

"It is," said Corvus from the altar.

"What is it?" I said. "Some book about the Dark Ones, I suppose? Their secret gospel or whatever?" I cast the spell to sense the presence of magic. All the items upon the altar radiated dark magic, but there was a powerful magical object in the alcove.

"It is called the Void Codex," said Corvus. I glanced back and saw him lift the book from its pedestal. "It was written in Germany sometime in the fifteenth century by a heretic priest who had founded a cult devoted to the Dark Ones. The wars of the Reformation wiped out his cult, but copies of his book survived and have circulated ever since. They did little harm until the High Queen's advent and the Conquest…"

"Because magic became far more common then," I said, sifting through the detritus on the shelves. It mostly seemed to be bloodstained cloths and old knives. I wondered how many people McCade had killed down here. I wondered what he had done with the bodies.

Suddenly I was glad I had not eaten McCade Foods canned meats in quite some time.

"Precisely," said Corvus. "The book became far more dangerous, and the High Queen banned it and ordered the destruction of any copies."

"Hard to do that on the Internet," I said, squatting down to examine the last shelf.

A scroll rested on the bottom shelf. I opened it up, and a surge of excitement went through me. Elven hieroglyphs covered the scroll, and I realized it was a spell. I didn't recognize the spell, but I did spot the hieroglyph for "mind" near the top of the scroll. If I lived through this, I could learn a new spell, another spell that I might use to free myself and Russell from Morvilind's grasp.

I stuffed it into my duffel bag, and realized that Corvus was still talking. Best not to mention this little discovery to him.

"The Inquisition has tried," said Corvus, closing the book and picking it up. "Anyone caught hosting, downloading, or reading the file is executed at once. They don't even bother with a Punishment Day video. They've also flooded with Internet with false copies, and track anyone who tries to download it."

"That's actually halfway clever," I said, pushing away some bloodstained rags, grateful that I was wearing gloves. "I think…"

I froze.

The tablet Morvilind wanted sat on the bottom shelf.

The damned thing looked so…tiny. I don't know what I expected. Morvilind had told me it weighed nine pounds, and stone is fairly dense, so it couldn't have been too big. Nevertheless I had been planning to steal it for weeks, and it loomed so large in my thoughts that it should have been at least as tall as the menhirs along the Warded Ways. Instead the tablet was about the size of both of my hands and two inches thick. It looked like a fancy bathroom tile, albeit one covered with cuneiform. Morvilind had said it was an Assyrian tablet, so I suppose the language was Assyrian. I vaguely remembered from the Marneys' church that the Assyrians had been bloodthirsty warriors and brutal conquerors in ancient days. Perhaps the Dark Ones had helped them with such conquests.

The tablet absolutely radiated dark magic. The stone was cool and dry, yet somehow gave off the sensation of rancid greasiness, even through my gloves. I felt an urge to fling it away from me, the same urge I would have felt if a spider had crawled up my bare arm. Yet for Russell's sake I had to deliver the damned thing to Morvilind.

I pulled off my makeshift backpack and opened it, drawing out a little roll of bubble wrap and another of duct tape. With a few quick motions I secured the tablet within the bubble wrap and tucked it into my pack. I didn't know if the dark magic upon the tablet made it more resistant to cracks than regular stone, but the thing was thousands of years old and I wasn't going to take chances. I pulled the straps over my shoulders and stood up. The extra weight of the tablet was uncomfortable, but not unbearable.

"What are you doing?" said Corvus.

I blinked. He had the Void Codex tucked under his left arm, its unadorned cover made of green leather. In his right hand he held his Shadowmorph blade, blacker than the marble beneath my shoes.

"The same thing you are," I said. "What I came here to do."

His eyes were hard and cold. "You came here to steal an artifact of dark magic? A relic of the Dark Ones themselves?"

I shrugged. "I came here to steal what I was hired to steal. I don't give a damn what my employer does with it."

"That thing is dangerous," said Corvus.

"You so sure of that?" I said. "Can you read Assyrian?"

"No."

I shrugged again, the straps digging into my shoulders. If I got out of here and Morvilind wanted me to steal another piece of rock, I would make sure to bring padded straps. "Then how do you know it's dangerous? For all you know, it's some old Assyrian king's recipe for sugar cookies."

"Because," said Corvus, "I can sense the dark power around the thing as well as you can."

"Not my problem," I said. "I don't intend to use it."

"Then you will merely sell it for money," said Corvus.

"Something like that," I said. I couldn't tell him the truth. Morvilind had been very clear about what would happen if I told anyone the details of our little "arrangement".

"Then you are a fool," said Corvus. "It is dangerous..."

"Don't lecture me," I snapped. "I don't want to hear any speeches about morality from an assassin who kills for money."

"We," said Corvus, his voice just shy of a growl, "are not assassins. The Shadow Hunters are..."

"Executioners, yes, yes, I know," I said. "But you don't do it for free, do you? I bet you get a little remuneration? Maybe a little honorarium? And the parasite inside you feeds off the life force of your victims, lets you do all kind of neat tricks. So don't claim to be an executioner or some sort of knight on a mission. You're a hired killer, plain and simple."

"The magic in that tablet is dangerous," said Corvus, his eyes hard and flat, "and it will destroy you if you attempt to use it."

"That's good news, then," I said. "If my employer uses it and makes his head explode, I'll be rid of him." I waved a hand at him. "You found your book, your Void Codex or whatever. Don't you have someone to assassinate?"

"I will not let you take that tablet to work evil elsewhere," said Corvus. "Or...yes, I see now. Has this been a game all along? Perhaps you belong to a rival cult, and you've come to steal McCade's artifact for your own high priest."

I burst out laughing. "Don't be an idiot. I didn't know these Dark Ones existed until about five minutes ago. Listen to me, Corvus. I don't care about the Dark Ones, I don't care about the Rebels, I don't care about the High Queen, I don't care about anything. All I care about is selling this tablet." For with that tablet, I could buy another piece of Russell's life from Morvilind's grasping, miserly hands.

"Then you are a mercenary fool," said Corvus. "I am not sure which is worse. At least the cultists of the Dark Ones have their faith, however mad and twisted. You, however, are heedless of the harm you could cause, and care nothing for anything except your money..."

"I have my own purpose," I said. "One a blood-drenched old murderer like you would never understand. Now. Go about your business and get out of my way."

"I will not let you leave with that tablet," said Corvus.

"Oh?" I said. "Are you going to stop me?"

"If I must," said Corvus.

I met his gaze without blinking. "Sure you can do that?"

He didn't say anything, the Shadowmorph sword motionless in his right hand.

He could stop me. In a fight, there was no way I could take him. I didn't have any spells that could harm him. Cloaking would be useless, since he already knew I was here. I didn't have any way of deflecting his lightning spells, and the thought of fighting him physically was ludicrous. The man had picked me up and sprinted over the Warded Way without breaking a sweat. Short of shooting him in the back of the head with a gun, there was absolutely no way I could overcome him.

But he didn't necessarily know that.

I met his gaze, forcing myself not to show any fear. My only way out of this was to bluff, and I did not dare show any weakness.

The silence stretched on and on.

"Well," I said at last, "what's it going to be?"

Corvus drew himself up and started to speak.

I never did find out what he intended to say.

Three loud clangs echoed through the black temple, ringing in my ears. I looked around in surprise, half-wondering if Corvus had somehow drawn a gun and shot at me. Yet the Shadow Hunter looked just as startled as I did.

Then my brain caught up with me, and I realized where I had heard that sound before.

It was the sound of a very expensive series of locks and bolts releasing.

The vault door was opening.

Corvus whirled, turning his back to me, and my training took over. I took three quick steps back, concealing myself between the massive circuit breaker boxes and the back of the alcove. The altar would block the view of the alcove, and anyone who entered the temple would see Corvus first.

Footsteps clicked against the marble floor. Three men, I thought, all of them wearing dress shoes. Had we triggered some sort of silent alarm in the temple? Though if McCade himself had summoned up those wraithwolves, he might have been linked to them with a spell. Perhaps he could even have seen through their eyes.

McCade's voice rang out, smooth and calm with his Midwestern accent.

"Well, well, well," said McCade. "A Shadow Hunter. I was wondering when you would show up. But, really, you are a most welcome guest. My lord requires sacrifices in exchange for his gifts. And you and your Shadowmorph will make a most welcome gift."

CHAPTER 10
HIGH PRIEST

I tensed, uncertain of what to do, my mind sorting potential plans. Though perhaps it was too late for a plan. McCade knew that we were here, and there was only one way out of the temple. I suppose I could open another rift way, but it would return to the edge of that chasm in the Shadowlands, and there was every chance the floating tentacle-thing was still lurking nearby. I would trade getting shot in the head for getting eaten by some horror from the Shadowlands.

"Paul McCade," said Corvus with contempt. "Come to grovel before the bloodstained altar of the horrors you worship as a false god?"

McCade laughed. "The legendary Shadow Hunters rather fail to live up to the legend. Isn't that a shame? All those stories about your prowess and cunning, how you can slip through the shadows and scale walls like an insect. All those stories, and you follow the laws like all the other ignorant rabble that bow before their portraits of the High Queen."

"The Dark Ones are older than the High Queen, McCade," said Corvus. "And far more dangerous. The High Queen might be a tyrant…"

"Don't be so elfophobic, Shadow Hunter," said McCade with amusement. "Or else you'll wind up on a Punishment Day video squealing like a pig."

"She might be a tyrant," said Corvus as if McCade had not spoken, "but concerning the Dark Ones her law is correct. The Dark Ones are dangerous…"

"Certainly they are dangerous, but the Dark Ones greatly reward those who serve them well," said McCade. "You have seen my mansion? I received all my wealth and power from our lord. My father founded this cult. He was working as a farmhand in South Dakota when he found a cult of the Dark Ones that had been active in the Black Hills since the days of the Aztecs. He joined the cult and brought them here to Milwaukee, along with the copy of the Void Codex which you are now manhandling. The secrets of the Dark Ones let the company rise to power and wealth. When my father died, I inherited the company…and I became the high priest of the cult."

"A fascinating story," said Corvus, "though I wonder why you are telling it to me."

"Isn't it obvious?" said McCade. He sounded as cheerful as if he was discussing a baseball game over beer. "You're not leaving here alive, Shadow Hunter. Neither you nor your little friend. Where is she, by the way? My pets told me that two of you entered here, a man and a woman. Where is she?"

"I came alone," said Corvus.

I blinked in surprise. I had expected Corvus to tell my location to McCade. Still, he might think me a wretched, mercenary thief, but that still made me better than a cultist of the Dark Ones. A weird little flicker of emotion went through me. Was it shame? Corvus was right about me. I was a wretched, mercenary thief. Not that I had any choice in the matter. Not that I had ever had any choice in the matter. If I had possessed the power…

The way things were going, I might not have the power to leave this room.

"How very chivalrous," said McCade. "Was she yours? Your little…pet? We'll have some fun with her, and then offer her to our lord. It will reward us with great power for her blood."

Had he been able to see me, I would have offered him a rude gesture.

"That presumes you can kill me," said Corvus.

"You're faster and stronger than we are," said McCade, "and that Shadowmorph blade of yours can cut through anything. You can also heal from nearly anything…but I imagine ten bullets through your chest and six through your head would prove a challenge for even the healing prowess of a Shadowmorph."

"Then," said Corvus, "why haven't you shot me already?"

"I wish to make you an offer," said McCade.

I inched forward a bit, peering around the edge of the circuit breaker boxes and into the temple proper. I spotted Corvus standing behind the altar. He had dropped the book and held his dark blade raised before him, his stance tense and ready. McCade waited below the dais, a .45 semi-automatic pistol in his hands. A lot of rich guys who had never served as men-at-arms don't know how to hold guns properly, but McCade held his weapon with a proper stance, both hands on the grip, his legs spread to handle the recoil. Two of his security men stood on either side of him, both holding identical weapons. All three of them kept their weapons trained at Corvus. As fast as he was, he couldn't dodge three competent shooters at once.

They hadn't noticed me yet, but after they killed Corvus, they would search the alcove.

I had to think of something clever. Like, right now. Could I open a rift way in time? No, the light would draw notice. And I might have been a mercenary thief, but I disliked the thought of leaving Corvus to die. He had saved my life from the wraithwolves, and he hadn't sold me out to McCade.

Maybe he expected me to do something clever.

But what?

"You should join us, Shadow Hunter," said McCade.

"And just why should I do that?" said Corvus.

"The Dark Ones are going to triumph," said McCade. "You know it, I know it, and even the High Queen herself knows it in the depths of her black heart. She has fought against the Dark Ones for centuries, but in the end they will prevail. The advent of the Dark Ones is at hand, and when they enter our world great rewards shall be given to their loyal followers…"

"Don't quote the Void Codex at me," said Corvus.

McCade laughed. "Would you prefer it in the original German?"

"I would prefer," said Corvus, "that you not weary my ears with lies in any language. There is only one God, and you have turned away from him to worship monsters."

"The superstitions of ignorant rabble, believed by fools for millennia," said McCade. "The Dark Ones are real, and they grant gifts of real power. Oh, well. If you will not join us, then you will make a worthy sacrifice to our lord…"

He said…something. A word, a name, a title, I'm not sure what. I heard the syllables, heard the sounds come out of his mouth, but when my mind tried to process them into a coherent word…

Pain exploded through my head, and I had to grab at the side of the metal circuit breaker box to keep my balance. I heard Corvus grunt and stagger back, and glimpsed the black lines of the Shadowmorph crawling over his face. McCade had spoken the name of whatever Dark One he worshipped, and even the mere sound of it had been like getting hit in the face.

"Our lord's name brings torment to those who are not among his chosen," said McCade. "Kill him."

The two security men circled around the altar from the left and the right, while McCade covered the center. Corvus ducked behind the altar, but that would only give him a few seconds at best. McCade and his two goons had Corvus boxed in. No matter what direction Corvus tried to attack, at least two guns would cover him. I didn't know whether a single bullet through the heart or brain would be enough to kill a Shadow Hunter, but I was sure that it would slow him enough so they could pump him full of lead at their leisure, and that would kill him.

Then they would kill me. At least, if I was lucky, they would kill me. There were all sorts of unpleasant things they could do to me first.

Unless...

My eyes moved to the circuit breaker boxes. One of them had a steel lever topped with a black rubber knob. Above the lever was a yellow sticker marked with WARNING in black letters, followed by several paragraphs of legalese. Morvilind's various tutors, alas, had not taught me the intricacies of modern electrical systems. However, I was willing to bet that the big WARNING lever would cut off power to the circuit breakers.

And if those circuit breakers connected to the lights, that would plunge the temple into darkness.

I stepped out of concealment, my duffel bag bouncing against my back, seized the lever in both hands, and pulled. At first it did not move, but it felt it start to give a little.

"Boss!" shouted one of the security men. "I see her! She's..."

"Cover the Hunter, you idiot!" snarled McCade.

The security man swung his gun around to point at me, and I yanked on the lever with all the strength I could muster, planting my shoes against the wall and shoving. The lever jerked down with a clunking noise, and I landed hard on my back, right atop my duffel bag. That hurt, though I was more concerned for the tablet.

The security man took aim, settling into a shooting stance, his legs spread, both hands coiled around the grip of his pistol. I rolled to the side, hoping to get to the meager cover of the shelves before he shot me to death.

Then the circuit breaker boxes let out an angry buzz, and the lights went out.

An instant later I heard the crack of a gunshot, followed by the high-pitched whine of a ricochet bouncing off the black wall. I scrabbled backwards in the darkness, ducking behind the shelf. I had never been shot, and I didn't really want to find out what it felt like. Both the security men started shouting, and I heard several more shots go off, the sharp cracks echoing off the stone walls.

"Stop shooting!" roared McCade. "You'll hit each other. Or me! Or you'll blunder into the summoning circle!" He snarled a phrase in the Elven language, and pale green light flared in the darkness. A trio of globes of sickly green light appeared over the altar, throwing dim radiance and harsh shadows everywhere.

As I had suspected, McCade could use some magic. That was bad.

On the other hand, he was an idiot, which was good. That light had marked out his position to Corvus. I suspected the Shadow Hunter could see far more clearly in the gloom than a normal man could.

Yet both McCade and his goons were handling themselves well. They began to move towards the altar, covering each other. If Corvus came at them, they could line up some clear shots and gun him down. Corvus needed a distraction if he was going to get McCade. I didn't have any weapons, or any real way of hurting them.

I did have some illusions, though.

I lifted my hand and worked the Masking spell, hiding the telltale light with my body. I didn't have enough time or concentration to do a detailed Mask, but in the dim light that didn't matter. I Masked myself as a facsimile of one of the security guards – the same black suit, muscular build, and close-cropped hair.

I made sure to alter my voice as well.

Then I took a deep breath, pushed away from the wall, and sprinted into the temple proper.

"There!" I shouted in my disguised voice. "He's there! Boss, he's there, by the door! Get him! He's running!"

The trick worked. In the dim light, McCade and his men mistook me for one of the guards. They whirled to face the vault door and started shooting, the muzzle flashes brilliant in the gloom. I kept running, slipped my duffel bag off my shoulders, took one more running stride, and spun as fast as I could as the Mask dissolved around me.

The bag hit the nearest security guard in the left temple. His head jerked back with an uncomfortable crunching sound, and he staggered towards the altar. I dropped the duffel bag, seized the barrel of his gun with my left hand, and drove the fingers of my right hand into his wrist. Normally, something like this wouldn't have worked, and I would have gotten shot in the head for my trouble. But I had managed to hit him hard, and the impact had stunned him. I wrenched the gun from his hand, got my fingers around the grip, and started shooting.

There were three rounds in the magazine, and I used them all. The first two hit him in the chest, and the third went into his forehead. The guard went sprawling in a limp heap to the ground, his blood gleaming in a dark pool beneath his head as it reflected McCade's ghostly light. McCade and the remaining guard whirled to face me. I threw the empty pistol in McCade's general direction and dove next to the altar just as they started shooting. Bullets whined off the altar, and I ducked next to the massive block of black marble. The surviving guard's gun clicked empty, and he cursed and reached into his jacket for another clip. I peered around the edge of the altar, wondering if I could do something to stun or disable the guard before he reloaded, wondering how many shots McCade had left in his weapon. He had fired five times? Six times? A gun like that usually held eight or nine rounds, so either way if he got a clear shot at me I was in trouble…

Corvus exploded out of the darkness, moving faster than I had yet seen him move.

The guard whirled towards him, fumbling with his gun, but Corvus was faster. The Shadowmorph blade plunged into the guard's chest and out his back without the slightest hint of resistance. The guard went limp, and the shadowy blade seemed to pulse in Corvus's hand, swelling and flickering with a peculiar dark glow as it drank away the guard's life. Corvus pulled the weapon free with a flick of his wrist and turned towards McCade.

McCade leveled his gun and shot Corvus twice. The Shadow Hunter stumbled as the bullets entered his chest and stomach. I didn't seen any exit wounds, which meant the rounds had lodged somewhere in his spine or his ribs, or they had deflected off a bone and bounced around his chest cavity. Either way he was badly injured. If the bullet had hit his heart, he was going to fall over dead.

Instead he shook his head and grimaced, and through the tattered ruins of his shirt and jacket I saw the spiraling black lines writhe over the muscles of his chest and belly, saw his flesh ripple and contort. I heard one metallic clink, and then another as the bullets fell out of him and bounced off the floor, as the life force he had stolen from the dead security guard healed the wounds that should have killed him.

McCade backed away, his eyes wide with fright.

"Paul McCade," said Corvus, striding forward as he raised his sword of dark force. "For possession of the Void Codex, for trafficking with the Dark Ones, for offering them sacrifices, I bear a decree commanding your execution. Have you anything to say?"

I moved towards the guard Corvus had killed, keeping my eyes on McCade. He fumbled his jacket for another clip, but there was no way he could reload and fire before Corvus reached him. Something mad and desperate flashed over his features as I went to one knee next to the guard and claimed his emptied gun.

McCade's lips peeled back from his face in a snarl, his features livid with fury. It was strange to see such rage upon his solemn face. Men like him did not raise their voices in anger. Men like him gave orders in soft, polite tones, and other men went to carry out violence in their name.

"I have this to say, Shadow Hunter, trained dog of the High Queen," said McCade. "You should have made me a better offer."

He whirled and ran. That was foolish. Corvus could run him down with ease. McCade would only run to…

The realization hit me.

"Corvus!" I shouted. "He's…"

McCade ran into the summoning circle. Harsh green light blazed up from the circle, the Elven hieroglyphs shining with ghostly green fire. Corvus cursed and sprinted towards the circle, but McCade threw out his arms and shouted his lord's name once more. Again I heard the string of syllables, the sequence of sounds that created a word, but again my mind refused to resolve it, and pain exploded through my head. Corvus stumbled as well, the black tattoo of the Shadowmorph crawling over his face.

"Behold!" screamed McCade, his voice a strange mixture of ecstasy and agony and joy and terrified horror. "Behold the glory of my lord! Behold the might of a Dark One!"

With those words, McCade…changed.

He grew, swelling to nearly twice the size, his expensive suit ripping apart as his flesh swelled. Even as he did, his form twisted and distorted, bulging muscle rippling over his limbs. His skin glistened with slime as it changed into a combination of leathery scales and an insect-like exoskeleton. Twitching spider's legs erupted from his sides, and a mane of barbed tentacles burst from his back and his head.

I had never seen anything like it. Just looking at him made my head hurt, just as McCade shouting the name of his Dark One lord had sent a stab of agony through my skull. His very form had become hideous and twisted, an abomination. Even the wraithwolves had something recognizable in them, something sane and understandable. The thing that McCade had become had neither.

He had been possessed by a Dark One.

"Die!" screamed McCade in a strange double voice. From his mouth, or at least the barbed orifice that had been his mouth, came two voices. One was the voice of Paul McCade, albeit distorted with pain and madness. The other…the other was a voice that sent little jagged pulses of agony through my head. It was as if every word the voice spoke was a name of a Dark One. "Die, worms! Die!"

The creature surged forward, pincers and tentacles reaching for Corvus. He leaped to the side, moving with the inhuman speed granted by his Shadowmorph, but McCade kept pace with him. One of the tentacles lashed across Corvus's chest, opening a gash and knocking him back several steps.

I grabbed the clip the security guard had been trying to load. I ejected the empty clip, slammed the new one into the gun, and took aim. A deep breath, and I emptied the clip into McCade, aiming for his…well, the thing that had been his torso. I suppose it was his center of gravity now. I wasn't the best shot, but McCade had gotten a lot bigger. All nine bullets tore into McCade, staggering him. He let out a hideous scream of rage and fury that sawed into my head, black slime spurting from the wounds. Yet it didn't slow him. He resumed his pursuit, his tentacles and pincers reaching for Corvus.

I looked around, frantic. Part of my mind pointed out that I could take the duffel bag and run, leaving Corvus to his fate. He had been willing to take the tablet, which would have condemned Russell to death. But he hadn't known that, had he? He thought he had been doing the right thing, and as annoying as it had been, I couldn't blame a man for that.

A more practical part of my mind pointed out that McCade had seen my face, that he would realize that I had stolen his tablet, and that I had just pissed him off by shooting him nine times. Even if I ran, once he finished Corvus, he would hunt me down and kill me.

If Corvus and I didn't kill McCade now, I was going to die.

But I had no idea how to kill him. He had shrugged off nine bullets, and I had no spells that could hurt him. I racked my brain, trying to think of an idea. I didn't know anything about the Dark Ones, save what I had learned today, but Morvilind had taught me a little about summoning spells. Summoning creatures from the Shadowlands took tremendous amounts of magical power. If the Dark Ones came from the Void beyond the Shadowlands, then presumably it would take even more power to call up a Dark One.

So where had McCade gotten that power?

I cast the spell to sense the presence of magic again. I still felt the dark power radiating from the tablet in my duffel bag, and the malevolent auras around the dagger and chalice upon the altar. I also sensed the tremendous power radiating from the circle. It had been latent before, but McCade had activated it by crossing the boundary.

It was identical to the power within the chalice, the dagger, and the tablet. I suspected McCade had used the items to open the way to the Void, to make contact with whatever Dark One he worshipped. To do so had required a spell of great power.

And like many spells of great power, it was fragile.

I needed the tablet. I didn't need the chalice or the dagger.

I seized both items from the altar and flung them into the circle. There was a snarling flash of ghostly green flame, and a howling nothingness appeared into the center of the circle, a void that swallowed the chalice and the dagger whole. A pulse of dark magic washed through the temple, and the floor shuddered and groaned. A ribbon of green fire burst from the circle and wrapped around McCade, and the hulking creature screamed. He staggered, his pincers and tentacles lashing at the air, and Corvus regained his balance, his sword of dark force coming up in guard.

The darkness and the green fire winked out, and McCade screamed again. He shrank, withering and diminishing, and the hideous creature vanished. In its place stood a naked, slightly overweight middle-aged man, his eyes bright with madness and pain, a keening scream coming from his lips.

The Dark One had been banished, and McCade had returned to his normal form.

Though it looked as if the Dark One had taken McCade's sanity.

Paul McCade screamed in fury, gibbering and laughing, and flung himself at Corvus.

He got maybe half a step before the dark blade lashed out, taking off McCade's head. The body collapsed at the Shadow Hunter's feet, while the head rolled down the stairs of the dais. Corvus looked at the corpse, breathing hard, and closed his eyes for a moment.

I took the opportunity to pick up my duffel bag, slinging it over my shoulders. It felt like the tablet was still intact. I doubt Morvilind would have been forgiving if I told him I had broken the tablet over the head of a security guard employed by a Dark One-possessed food magnate.

Corvus opened his eyes, his shadow-filled gaze falling upon me.

"Be sure to get the bullets," I said.

"Bullets?" he said.

"The ones that…uh, popped out of you when you healed," I said. "Once Homeland Security starts investigating McCade's death, they might use the blood on the bullets to trace you." His wounds had vanished, healed by the dark power of his Shadowmorph, and a grim thought occurred to me. "When you drank McCade's life, did you pull in any of the…essence of the Dark One inside him?"

"No," said Corvus. He lowered his hand, and the sword dissipated into nothingness, the lines of his tattoo across his chest going still. He knelt and retrieved the bullets. "You had banished the Dark One back to the Void, and I could kill him without fear."

"Oh," I said. "Well. Good."

"Thank you for my life, Katerina Annovich," said Corvus.

"What?"

"I might have been able to take both guards," said Corvus, "and McCade before he transformed. But once he summoned his Dark One, I would not have been able to overcome him. If you had not acted, I would have died."

I snorted. "Don't read too much into it. If they had killed you, I would have been next on the list."

"Nevertheless," said Corvus. "You could have abandoned me several times, but you did not. Thank you."

I shrugged, uncomfortable. I'm not used to being thanked for anything. "Well…you saved my life a couple of times. Guess that makes us even."

"The tablet," said Corvus. "Are you still going to take it?"

I tensed. "Are you going to stop me?"

"No." He watched me for a moment. "But I urge you to leave it behind. You've seen the kind of harm it can wreak. McCade must have used it to help contact his Dark One."

"I can't," I said.

"If it is about money," said Corvus, "I will pay you to…"

"It's not about money," I said. I dared not tell him the truth. But he had saved my life. "I…have to do this. I have to steal this stupid thing."

"Why?" said Corvus.

"Because I have to," I said. "I don't want to use it, and I'm not going to sell it. I just…I have to do this. There will be consequences if I do not."

"Consequences?" said Corvus, and then he nodded. "Ah. Someone has a hold over you. Someone you care about will suffer if you don't deliver the tablet. A lover, perhaps, or a child or a sibling."

"Something like that," I said. "I…really can't tell you more. Don't ask, because I can't tell you."

Corvus stared at me for a moment longer, and then nodded.

"Want to get out of here?" he said.

"Oh, God," I said. "I thought you'd never ask."

###

Despite the death of the host, the gala was still going strong, both the main party in the glassed-in courtyard and the drug-fueled revels in the hidden room. Sneaking through the hidden room proved easy enough, but a man in a bloody tuxedo and a woman in a dirty cocktail dress, cargo pants, and dusty running shoes couldn't go through the courtyard without drawing notice.

So we went out the window and into the muggy night. We cut across the vast lawn, following a route that avoided the security cameras, and returned to the street. No signs of alarm came from the mansion.

We had gotten away clean, at least so far.

"I guess this is where we part ways," I said as we reached the sidewalk. "Thanks again."

"I still owe you something of a debt," said Corvus. "I wish to repay it."

"No," I said. "No, you don't owe me anything. Just don't kill me and we'll call it even."

He reached into a pocket of his tattered coat and handed me a business card.

"What, the Shadow Hunters have business cards?" I said. "Call 1-800-555-KILL to arrange an execution?" It was the business card of a coffee shop on Wisconsin Avenue.

"Meet there at noon in ten days," said Corvus, "and I shall repay you then. If you wish."

I slipped the card into my pocket. "Maybe. Bye, Corvus. Thanks for not killing me."

He smiled, gave me a mocking little salute, and vanished into the muggy darkness. I started walking as well, and then broke into a jog as soon as I was out of sight of the mansion. I had stashed my motorcycle off the street a few blocks away, and I climbed atop it, fired up the engine, and got the hell out of there.

It was about two in the morning by the time I got back to my apartment. I locked the door behind me, dropped the duffel bag on the floor, and leaned my forehead against the wall for a moment, shivering. The reaction always hit me after a job. I had almost been killed any number of times in the last few hours, and I had seen things that would leave me with nightmares.

Oh, but I had gotten lucky.

If I had screwed up even once, if I hadn't made a deal with Corvus, I would have gotten killed. And if I had gotten killed, Russell would die.

The shaking got worse.

I headed to the bathroom, pulling off my clothes and dumping them on the floor. I turned on the shower and sat beneath it, my legs drawn up to my chest, my head pressed against my knees, and I sat that way until the shaking stopped.

CHAPTER 11
FIGHT ANOTHER DAY

The next morning I brought my motorcycle to a stop in front of Morvilind's mansion. I peeled off my jacket and draped it over the handlebars, setting my helmet on the seat. I tucked the wrapped tablet under my arm and headed up to the front door.

"Miss Moran." Rusk awaited me by the doors, stern and formal in his red coat. "Lord Morvilind desires your presence in the library at once."

"Yeah, I guessed," I said. "Well, you can get on with escorting me there."

Rusk shook his head. "You are to go alone, Miss Moran."

I frowned. "Why?"

Rusk shrugged. "I do not question Lord Morvilind's commands, Miss Moran. I merely obey. Perhaps his lordship has finally tired of your smart remarks."

"I'm the very soul of courtesy," I said, but a fresh shiver of fear went down my spine. Maybe Morvilind had decided to dispose of me, and didn't want Rusk as a witness. Though if Morvilind did want to kill me, he wouldn't care if his domestic servants witnessed the deed. None of them would dare betray him.

Rusk only grunted and stepped aside.

I made my way to Morvilind's library. It had not changed since my last visit, though some of the relics and artifacts upon the tables had been rearranged. Morvilind stood before the table with the three computer monitors, clad in the gold-trimmed black robe of an Elven archmage and the red cloak of an Elven noble.

All three monitors displayed reports of Paul McCade's death.

"In shocking news," said one of the talking heads in the news report,

"Paul McCade, CEO of McCade Foods, was found murdered in his lakeside mansion. A spokesman for Homeland Security has confirmed that McCade was killed during his annual Conquest Day gala with the honorable Duke Tamirlas of Milwaukee himself in attendance. Homeland Security has released no details to the public at this time, and…"

Morvilind tapped the keyboard with a bony finger, silencing the video.

I knelt and bowed my head. "My lord Morvilind."

"Nadia Moran," said Morvilind in his deep rasp. "Rise."

I stood as Morvilind's cold blue eyes considered me. He always looked so old, almost withered, as if a stiff breeze could knock him over. Yet I knew he could kill me with a thought, that he could destroy the entire mansion around us with a crook of his finger.

"My lord," I said, holding out the wrapped tablet. "As you commanded."

Morvilind took the tablet and gestured, working a minor spell. The brown paper and the bubble wrap crumbled into nothingness, revealing the tablet. Morvilind turned it over, examining the inscriptions. At last a faint smile went over his thin lips.

"Of course," he said. "I had not considered that possibility. Interesting indeed."

"Then you are satisfied, my lord?" I said. "I have completed your task?"

"You have, child," said Morvilind, setting the tablet next to one of his computer monitors. He reached into his sleeve and drew out a small, crystalline object.

It was the vial holding my heart's blood.

"My lord?" I said in alarm.

"The task was completed satisfactorily, as I expected," said Morvilind. "Though now I have a few questions for you."

He cast a spell before I could react. The vial of blood chimed, and I felt a tightness in my veins. He had laid a spell of mind magic over me, a compulsion he had used on me before. While the spell lasted, I would have to answer any questions honestly.

"It is curious," said Morvilind, "that I sent you to steal the tablet. Do I not instruct you to remain quiet and unnoticed?"

My limbs tightened at the question. The spell felt like my skin was shrinking against my bones, and it compelled me to answer.

"Yes, my lord," I said.

"Indeed," said Morvilind. "Did you kill Paul McCade?"

"No," I said.

"Who did?" said Morvilind.

"A Shadow Hunter," I said.

Morvilind rolled the vial between his fingers, his cold blue eyes regarding me without blinking. I had the distinct feeling he was weighing my life, deciding if it would be of any further value to him.

"What did you tell him?" said Morvilind.

"I told him nothing about you," I said. "Only that I had been hired to steal the tablet."

"Elaborate."

"He was there to kill McCade," I said. "McCade had a copy of the Void Codex."

Morvilind grimaced. "Of course he did. Continue."

"The decree of execution said that if McCade had a copy of the Codex, then the Hunter would kill him," I said. "McCade did, the Hunter killed him, and…that was that."

"Who arranged the decree of execution with the Hunters?"

"Duke Tamirlas," I said. "At least that's what the Hunter said. I don't know if he told me the truth."

"I see," said Morvilind. He considered this for a moment. "You told the Hunter nothing of me?"

"No," I said. "No details."

"What did you tell him?" said Morvilind.

"We made a deal," I said. "He helped me to steal the tablet, and I helped him find the Codex. Then we parted ways."

"Interesting," said Morvilind. "The Shadow Hunters have always hunted the followers of the Dark Ones and destroyed their relics, even before the Conquest."

Curiosity overrode my fear. "Before the Conquest?"

"The society of the Shadow Hunters dates back at least forty-five centuries to the rise of Sargon of Akkad," said Morvilind. "A short time to an Elf, but a large span of recorded human history. It is irrelevant at the moment. Why did the Hunter let you depart with the tablet?"

"I saved his life when McCade called up his Dark One," I said. "The Hunter seemed…disinclined to argue about the tablet after the fight."

"Mmm," said Morvilind. "Did you seduce him?"

"No!" I said. "Well, I did kiss him…"

Morvilind raised a pale eyebrow.

"It was part of a disguise," I said. "To hide from the guards. I did not seduce him. And we didn't do anything but kiss."

"Very well," said Morvilind, and he waved his hand. The tightness vanished from my skin as he released his spell. "You have completed this task to my satisfaction. You may depart for now. I shall summon you when I require your services again."

He started to turn.

"Wait," I said.

Morvilind stopped, those cold eyes falling upon me.

"Why did you want that tablet?" I said.

Morvilind said nothing.

"It's a thing of the Dark Ones," I said. "The old Assyrians must have worshipped them. The Inquisition kills anyone dealing with the Dark Ones, the Shadow Hunter said so. Are you…"

Morvilind sighed and tapped the vial with a finger.

And pain exploded through me like a storm, so shocking and sudden that I screamed. My legs collapsed beneath me, and I fell hard upon my side, my head bouncing off the polished floor and sending another wave of agony through me. Morvilind gestured, and the power of his magic seized me and lifted me off the floor. I screamed again as his spell threw me into the air, and I feared he would smash me against the ceiling.

Instead he released the spell, and I tumbled towards the floor. The thirty-foot fall might kill me, or it might break every bone in my body and leave me crippled. At the last minute Morvilind's magic caught me again, and I hung suspended and upside down, floating a few feet above the floor.

Through it all Morvilind watched me with the same calm, slightly bored expression. He looked like a man attending to a tedious but necessary chore. I hung upside down for a few moments, breathing hard and trying to keep the tears from eyes.

At last Morvilind stepped closer.

"Nadia Moran," said Morvilind in a quiet voice. "I will only tell you this once. Never mention the Inquisition to me again. Never question me about the Dark Ones again. If you do, I will not let your brother die. I will kill him myself in front of your eyes. It will take days, and I will make sure that he curses your name before at last I grant him death. Do you understand?"

I nodded.

"Say it," said Morvilind.

"Yes," I croaked.

He sighed and tapped the vial again.

I spent a bad few minutes screaming.

"Yes, my lord," I said when I could form words again.

He crooked his finger, and I spun around and landed in a heap at his feet.

"You may depart," he said. "Await me at the Marneys' home tomorrow. It is time for your brother's yearly cure spell."

"Yes, my lord," I said. I dragged myself to my feet and left.

###

The next day I took my motorcycle to the Marneys' house.

James wore his old dress uniform, and Lucy her nicest dress. Russell wore a suit that was too big for him, but he would grow into it. Morvilind arrived with a half-dozen of his human servants. After he had deigned to accept the Marneys' greetings, he cast the cure spell.

It was a work of tremendous power, drawing upon all of the elements and sources of magical power I could not identify. The spell was complex beyond my ability to comprehend. Silver light and golden fire blazed around his hands and sank into Russell. When he finished, Russell looked…stronger, a little less pale, a little less sickly.

Morvilind was a hard and ruthless man, but he kept his word.

He left once the spell was complete.

Russell was fourteen. That meant Morvilind needed to cast the healing spell six more times before he was completely cured. That meant I had six years left. I had to obey Morvilind for six more years until he cured Russell of the frostfever.

I just had to stay alive for six more years.

Or find the power to cure Russell myself and break free of Morvilind.

That night I sat with a cigarette and smoked with James.

"Russell looks better every year," said James. "When Lord Morvilind first brought him to us, I feared that he might not live to reach his tenth birthday."

I nodded, watching the smoke curl away into the night.

"Your work for Lord Morvilind," said James. "It is dangerous, isn't it? You've got the look."

"Look?" I said, startled. "What, do I have lettuce in my teeth?"

"No," said James. "The thousand yard stare. The men-at-arms would come back from the Shadowlands with that look."

We sat in silence for a while.

"This was a bad one," I said at last. "I can't tell you about it. But this…it almost didn't go well."

"It's a good thing you're doing, Nadia," said James.

"It is?" I said. If he knew the truth about me, he wouldn't say that.

"Your brother's alive because of what you're doing," said James. "When things get hard, that's what you have to remember."

I nodded. I hoped he was right.

###

Several days later I walked unnoticed through the lunchtime crowd on Wisconsin Avenue, my mind focused upon my new spell.

No one noticed me.

I grinned. That was the point.

The scroll I had found in McCade's temple had been a spell of mind magic and illusion, a spell called Occlusion. It didn't turn me invisible like a Cloak, or disguise me as someone else like a Mask. Instead, the Occlusion spell made me…unnoticeable. People simply didn't notice that I was there. So long as I did nothing aggressive, no one paid any attention to me. It wouldn't work around another wizard, but I had been in many situations where the Occluding spell would have come in handy.

I stepped into the coffee shop, released the spell, and looked around. It was a cozy sort of place, with wooden chairs and tables and a variety of junk pinned to the wall as some sort of art. Most of the customers were office workers stopping in for lunch or a snack.

Corvus sat at one of the tables, waiting for me. He wore a denim jacket, T-shirt, jeans, and his oversized sunglasses, and a pair of cardboard cups waited on the table before him. He rose as I approached and drew out a chair for me. I blinked in surprise at the archaic gesture, but sat anyway.

"You even wear those things inside?" I said as Corvus sat.

"The Shadowmorph does not like the sun," said Corvus.

"Or fashion," I said.

He smiled a little at that. "I am surprised you came."

"So am I," I said. "I half-expected that this would be a trap to kill me." In fact I had circled the building three times while Occluded, looking for signs of an ambush, but had found nothing.

"No," said Corvus. "I keep my word."

"I think I know that now," I said. "So. What did you want to talk about?"

"I repay my debts," said Corvus, reaching into his coat. He withdrew an envelope and handed it to me. I opened it and my eyes got wide. It held hundred-dollar bills, a lot of them.

"What's this?" I said.

"Half the bounty for the decree," said Corvus. "You earned it. I would have failed if not for your help."

I hesitated. This was blood money. Stealing was one thing. Killing people for money was something else.

But I really could use the money.

I tucked the envelope into my purse.

"There is a card with a phone number in the envelope as well," said Corvus. "If you need my aid, call that number."

"Giving me your phone number on a first date?" I said. "Little forward, isn't it?"

He didn't even blink at that. "Technically, this would be the second date."

"Robbery and infiltration do not count as a date," I said.

Corvus shrugged. "I am not familiar with modern standards of courtship. There is something else I can do for you."

"What?" I said.

He raised a hand. I flinched, fearing that he was about to cast a spell, but he only reached out and touched me on the forehead. It drew an odd glance from a passing couple. As he did, I felt a surge of magical energy, and the symbols and patterns of a spell burned themselves into my mind.

A spell. He had just given me the knowledge of a spell. It was the spell he used to conjure globes of lightning.

"Why…why did you do that?" I said.

"Because," said Corvus. "You saved my life, and it is an appropriate gift. You have no magical means of defending yourself. Now you do."

"Thank you," I said. "I…thank you." It was a tremendous gift.

He rose. "Take care of yourself, Katerina Annovich. Don't follow any more strange men into alleys."

I imitated the mocking little salute he had given me in the temple. "You have my solemn promise. Corvus…thank you. Really. You don't know how useful this will be for me."

"I can guess," Corvus said, and then left.

Later I sat in my Duluth Car Company sedan, and I cast the spell. A little snarling globe of lightning appeared over my fingers, and I smiled and dismissed it. Corvus had indeed given me a powerful gift.

Perhaps I could put it to good use.

For I was still alive, and Russell needed only six more healing spells. Russell was still alive, and I had survived my latest mission from Morvilind.

For now, that was victory enough.

EPILOGUE

Corvus stood in a New York City penthouse, finishing his report.

The Firstborn of the Shadow Hunters sat by the window, gazing at Manhattan's skyline as he listened. He looked about sixty, thin and tough and wiry as an old tree, but he was older than sixty, far older.

"This Katerina Annovich," said the Firstborn at last, "you do not think she is a servant of the Dark Ones?"

"No," said Corvus, thinking of the strange gray-eyed thief. "I suspect she is being coerced. Likely a cult of the Dark Ones is holding her family captive, using them to compel her obedience."

"She knew illusion magic," said the Firstborn. For a moment the lines of his Shadowmorph stirred against his seamed face. "Someone must have taught it to her."

Corvus nodded.

"Find her," said the Firstborn, "and keep watch over her. She might be the key." The ancient man looked up at him. "This is vital, Corvus. Find her. If we can find her, perhaps we can find her master…and strike the greatest blow against the Dark Ones since the High Queen was driven from her homeworld. Go with my blessing, my son."

Corvus bowed and strode to the elevator, thinking of the gray-eyed thief. He hoped she wouldn't need the spell he had given her. He hoped he could find her before the Rebels or the Archons or the cultists of the Dark Ones did.

The woman who called herself Katerina Annovich was in far more danger than she realized.

THE END

Thank you for reading CLOAK GAMES: THIEF TRAP. Look for Nadia's next adventure, CLOAK GAMES: FROST FEVER, to appear in 2015.

ABOUT THE AUTHOR

Standing over six feet tall, Jonathan Moeller has the piercing blue eyes of a Conan of Cimmeria, the bronze-colored hair a Visigothic warrior-king, and the stern visage of a captain of men, none of which are useful in his career as a computer repairman, alas.He has written the DEMONSOULED series of sword-and-sorcery novels, the TOWER OF ENDLESS WORLDS urban fantasy series, THE GHOSTS series about assassin and spy Caina Amalas, the COMPUTER BEGINNER'S GUIDE sequence of computer books, and numerous other works. Visit his website at: http://www.jonathanmoeller.com

Printed in Great
Britain
by Amazon